TWISTED TALES FROM SHAKESPEARE
has a subtitle supplied by the author for the benefit (it is only
fair to assume) of his readers: "In which Shakespeare's best-
known plays are presented in a new light, the old light having
blown a fuse, together with introductions, questions, appen-
dices, and other critical apparatus intended to contribute to a
clearer misunderstanding of the subject."

RICHARD ARMOUR holds a Harvard PhD, and has taught at
the University of Texas, Northwestern University, Wells College, the University of Freiburg, the University of Hawaii,
Scripps College, and the Claremont Graduate School. He is
still Professor of English at the latter two. For other works,
please see the last page of this book.

D0830528

Twisted Tales from Shakespeare

Richard Armour

Twistfully Illustrated by Campbell Grant

McGraw-Hill Book Company, Inc.
New York   Toronto   London

LIBRARY OF CONGRESS CATALOG CARD NUMBER: 57–10901

PUBLISHED BY THE MC GRAW-HILL BOOK COMPANY, INC.

PRINTED IN THE UNITED STATES OF AMERICA

1920 FGRFGR   832

ISBN 07-002251-8

Dedicated to

the memory of Shakespeare,
which was certainly better than mine,
and to all those who,
having given or taken a required course in Shakespeare,
know that it is more blessed to give.

Acknowledgment

Incredible as it may seem, the author once
studied under that great Shakespeare scholar,

GEORGE LYMAN KITTREDGE

Contents

General Introduction

The Plays

Appendices

GENERAL INTRODUCTION

William Shakespeare, later known as the Beard of Avon, was born in 1564, on April 21, 22, or 23, and all his life kept people guessing. His mother was of gentle birth, but his father, who came of yeoman stock, was born the hard way. The house in which William saw the light is much the same today as it was then, except for the admission charge.*

Shakespeare grew up in the little town of Stratford-on-Avon, learning small Latin and less Greek, according to Ben Jonson, probably because he was busy amassing the largest English vocabulary until Noah Webster. For a time he worked for his father, a glover. He was a dreamy lad, which explains the unusual number of four- and six-finger gloves to be found in Stratford antique shops. Subsequently he was bound to a butcher, an awkward situation that kept his nose to the chopping block.

Much of his good taste Shakespeare inherited from his father, who once held the position of ale-taster for the town of Stratford. Young Will made the local team and met the Bidford Sippers in a spirited contest, winning his liter. According to Legend, the chief source of information about

* *Actually Shakespeare was not born in the Birthplace but in the Museum, a fact which he found embarrassing and kept secret from all but his closest friends.*

Shakespeare's youth, it took him two days to get home from Bidford, which was only a short walk but a long way on hands and knees.

When he was eighteen, Shakespeare met Anne Hathaway, who was eight years older and had begun to give up hope. What he saw in Anne is not known, but he may have admired her thatched roof, as so many have since. At any rate it gave him a good excuse for getting unbound from the butcher. Shakespeare's friends could see no reason for his rushing into marriage, but William and Anne could. Their daughter, Susanna, was born six months later.

Within two years, Shakespeare left for London—alone. Anne had given birth to twins, and there was no telling what she would do next. Moreover, he was accused of poaching something in a deer park, and it wasn't an egg.

Between 1585 and 1592 little is known of Shakespeare. These are the Lost Years, a period fraught with mystery and much more frustrating than the Lost Weekend. It may be that Shakespeare went into a deep sleep, like Rip Van Winkle, or wandered around in a daze, unaware of the execution of Mary Queen of Scots, the defeat of the Spanish Armada, and the introduction of the Irish potato. One authority, believing that Shakespeare must have been doing something of which he was ashamed, conjectures that he was a schoolteacher. This gave him access to the library, where he surreptitiously copied the plots of old plays for future use.

Some credence is given to the theory that Shakespeare during this period was holding horses outside a theater.* After eight years, he became one of the most experienced horse-

* *Unless they were held, they went inside to watch the play.*

4

holders in London. It was at this time that he began to write, holding the reins in one hand and a pen in the other. His earliest history plays were on the reins of Henry VI and Richard III, internal evidence being the famous line in the latter play, "A horse! A horse! My kingdom for a horse!" a cry which Shakespeare must often have heard from departing theatergoers on rainy nights.

Shakespeare was very versatile. Besides being a successful playwright, he was an actor and part owner of the theater. Once when they were short of scenery he painted himself green and played a tree. When not otherwise occupied, he sold tickets at the box office and souvenir programs in the aisles. This gave rise to the theory that there were six William Shakespeares, additional evidence being the six signatures in the British Museum, each spelled a different way. But there were actually only two: the Man and the Myth.

Several times Shakespeare acted in plays at the court of Queen Elizabeth, but the Queen was too busy watching Essex to notice. When King James came to the throne, Shakespeare was made one of the King's Men, a company of actors who had the right to protection from the King after a bad performance. Shakespeare never really excelled as an actor, but since he wrote the lines it was easy for him to learn them.

This was Merrie England, and Shakespeare had a gay time in London, his wife and children being in Stratford. He was often seen at the Mermaid Tavern, imbibing with Ben Jonson and the sons of Ben, who were sent to watch out for their father and carry him home. But his favorite pub was the Temple Bar. "Drink to me only with thine eyes," Ben was fond of saying, but Shakespeare knew he didn't mean a word

The Queen was busy

of it. "O rare Ben Jonson," he would remark, clinking canikins with his friend and quaffing the good English ale.*

In his last years, having had his fun, Shakespeare returned to Stratford and lived with his wife. When he died, he bequeathed her his second-best bed, the one with the broken springs and the crack in the headboard. Who got his number one bed is a dark secret.

Over Shakespeare's grave is an inscription that says: "Curst be he that moves my bones." So far as is known, the bones have never been moved in all these years. It is possible, of course, that this book may make Shakespeare turn over in his grave, but in that case he will have moved them himself.

* *No matter how rare Ben was to start with, by the end of the evening he was usually well done, in fact completely stewed.*

The theater of Shakespeare's day was modeled on the medieval innyard, as may be seen by the sign over the entrance, reading "Inne." There was no roof over the center part, which was occupied by "groundlings," poor people anxiously watching for rain clouds. There were also no seats in this part of the theater, and even at unpopular plays there was standing room only. Some spectators sat in galleries, around the sides, while the wealthy, the influential, and the nearsighted sat on the stage.

The first theater was very sensibly called the Theater.* The most famous theater, however, was the Globe, an octagonal building especially suited to Shakespeare's many-sided genius. Shakespeare was co-owner of the Globe, which burned down in 1613 when a cannon, shot off to awaken the spectators, set fire to the thatch.

The front stage was surrounded on three sides by the audience, which would have made it hard for John Barrymore, playing Hamlet, to show only his good profile. Separated from the front stage by a curtain was a rear stage. The curtain could be drawn to disclose a lady's bedchamber, a monk's cell, or a tomb, depending on whether the occupant was male or female, alive or dead. Above the stage was a balcony for balcony scenes, and still higher was a place for letting down angels and drawing up pitchers of ale. On the stage itself were numerous trapdoors, used when actors went to Hell.†

* *This was characteristic of Shakespeare's era, when they called a spade a spade.*

† *If a trapdoor wasn't securely fastened, an actor might be cut off in the midst of a soliloquy.*

7

Angels and ale pitchers

To the rear of the rear stage were tiring rooms, where actors grew weary from putting on and taking off costumes. At either side of the front stage were doors. These, according to scholars who have given their lives to a study of the Elizabethan theater, were used to go in and out of.

Admission to the theater ranged from a penny, for standing room in the yard, to three pennies, for a good seat in the gallery, tax included. This was cheaper than bearbaiting, because you didn't have to bring bait.

In Shakespeare's day people came to the theater to escape from the sordid realities of daily life and to relax. Nothing relaxed them so much as to see Hamlet running his sword through Laertes, Macduff carrying around Macbeth's head, Romeo falling dead in Juliet's bier,* and Othello smothering

* See, in Richard III, *the drowning of Clarence in a butt of malmsey.*

8

Desdemona.* It was sometimes difficult for them to decide, however, whether to spend the afternoon relaxing at the theater or at a public execution.

℘ Shakespeare's Development

Shakespeare didn't become a great dramatist overnight. But friends would occasionally exclaim, "By my troth, Will, thou'rt looking great," and his hopes would rise. As he wrote in *Twelfth Night*, "Some are born great, some achieve greatness, and some have greatness thrust upon them." With three possibilities, he felt he had a good chance. However, he resigned himself to the fact that he would not be called Immortal Shakespeare until after his death.

Shakespeare's first play, *A Comedy of Errors*, was so full of mistakes it was laughable.† But he was good-humored about it and promised to do better as soon as he got into his Second Period. His next plays were *Titus Andronicus*, in which the characters are bathed in blood, and *The Two Gentlemen of Verona*, in which the characters are bathed offstage, much to the disappointment of the audience. The best the defenders of Shakespeare can say is that "they are probably the work of several hands," only two of which can be the Bard's. As one critic has said of these early works, "The characterization is

---

* *At a good Elizabethan tragedy, the stage was strewn with rushes in the first act and with corpses in the fifth.*

† *The plot involves two sets of identical twins. Instead of ending in utter confusion, as so many Elizabethan comedies do, it begins that way.*

usually superficial, the psychology seldom subtle, and the dialogue inclined to be stiff, artificial, and overlong." Thus they are admirably suited for study in schools and colleges.

As Shakespeare developed, his true genius began to appear. Wisely, he wrote more and more blank verse, which readers could fill in themselves, and passages of sheer poetry which had to be read several times before it was clear that they could not be understood. In tragedies like *Romeo and Juliet* and comedies like *As You Like It* he so completely altered his borrowed plots that for many years he was given credit for inventing them. Maturing in characterization, he created in Romeo the first of his heroes to rise above himself, a feat made necessary by Juliet's unwillingness to climb down from her balcony.

Increasingly Shakespeare's concepts, which had been green and hard, ripened. His outlook on life deepened in *Hamlet*, *Macbeth*, and *King Lear*, and in *A Midsummer Night's Dream* it reached Bottom. Nor should we fail to mention Falstaff, in *Henry IV*, a well-rounded character, in fact a fascinating study in obesity.* Falstaff was such a large man that he slopped over into *Henry V* and *The Merry Wives of Windsor*. Reference should also be made to the profundity of his portrayal of Julius Caesar, who figures prominently in *Julius Caesar*, and to his treatment of Cassius, whose lean and hungry look suggests that he was treated none too well.

In his last plays, Shakespeare, who had scaled the heights, began to pick his way downward. *The Winter's Tale* is a tragicomedy, a wry jest that Shakespeare played on the scholars, who previously could put all of his plays into one

* *When he was wounded in battle, it took eight men to carry him off, two in front and six in the rear.*

category or the other. *The Tempest,* which tells of a shipwreck in the region of Bermuda, is full of tropical allusions and memorable lines, none of which come to mind at the moment. And *Cymbeline* contains one of Shakespeare's loveliest characters, Imogen, such a good woman and perfect wife that most critics consider her implausible. Tennyson, a Victorian with high standards of womanhood, died while reading about her, with a smile on his face.

Shakespeare's *Henry VIII* is thought by some to have been his last play. At least all agree that Henry VIII was the last Henry. Scholars suspect that Shakespeare collaborated with Fletcher, writing every other line. They could determine which lines are Shakespeare's and which are Fletcher's if only they knew who wrote the first one. But this bit of information, like his whereabouts during the Lost Years and who got his number one bed, Shakespeare carried to his grave. It now becomes evident why his bones cannot be moved. There isn't room.*

* *In the foregoing discussion no mention has been made of such plays as* King John, Richard II, Coriolanus, Pericles, *and* Timon of Athens. *On the theory that the less said about them the better, saying nothing is best of all.*

the plays

ḣAMLeᴛ

Introduction

Hamlet is a tragedy of revenge. Shakespeare was obviously getting back at somebody. It is a sad work of his maturity, possibly of his Blue Period, and he must have known what he was doing, even if the reader doesn't. Critics agree that Shakespeare's apprenticeship was behind him, which means that he could now write plays in a room by himself, without being overseen * by an Established Playwright.

Evidently Hamlet is based on an earlier play that got lost or was destroyed by Shakespeare after he cribbed from it. In this earlier play, the father's name is Ham and the son is Hamlet, or little Ham. Instead of wearing a suit of armor, the ghost is clad in a nightgown, having walked in his sleep all the way from Hell.†

Shakespeare's hand can be seen throughout the present play. At any rate, his fingerprints are all over the First Quarto (Q1), whereas they have not yet been detected in the First Folio

* Which is vastly different from being overlooked.
† When played in modern dress, the ghost wears pajamas.

(F1), *which was printed seven years after his death. Footprints on the title page remain a mystery.*

Some scholars maintain that in creating the character of Hamlet, Shakespeare was actually depicting himself, a person who could never make up his mind, liked to deliver long speeches when no one was listening, and was always poking his sword through the curtains to discourage eavesdropping. The fact that he named his only son Hamnet, even before he wrote the play, bolsters this belief, besides furnishing further proof that Shakespeare was never much good at spelling.* This same theory holds that Queen Gertrude is really Queen Elizabeth, which would mean that Elizabeth is the mother of Shakespeare and would lead to a complete reevaluation of the Virgin Queen.

* *Another indication of greatness. See Chaucer.*

The part of Hamlet has been played, in recent years, by such actors as John Barrymore, Leslie Howard, John Gielgud, and Sir Laurence Olivier, all of them capable of looking exceedingly melancholy, especially when someone in the audience gets up and leaves. Barrymore is known for his profile, Howard for his forehead, Gielgud for his voice, and Olivier for his wife.* People who are old enough to have seen John Barrymore's Hamlet feel superior to those who have not, but fortunately they grow fewer each year.

Hamlet is unquestionably Shakespeare's magnum opus, *of enormous interest to scholars and critics who would otherwise have been forced to seek honest employment. Hailed by Goethe, Schlegel, Coleridge, and Others,† it was written for the ages ‡ and will be read as long as there are teachers to require it.*

---

* *Mention should also be made of Maurice Evans, who is known for the way he can lose himself in a part, and sometimes in the scenery.*
† *To quote from any one of these, "Hail!"*
‡ *From twelve to sixteen.*

Hamlet sees a ghost

Hamlet, the Prince of Denmark, is known as the Melancholy Dane, capable of depressing anyone within sight or sound of him. The reason he mopes around all day is that his father has died and his father's brother has inherited both the throne and the Queen. Thus the new King, who had been Hamlet's uncle, is now his stepfather as well, and relations are becoming both strained and numerous. The King and Queen try to get Hamlet to stop mourning the death of his father and to take off his "inky cloak," on which as a student at Wittenberg he apparently kept wiping his pen. But Hamlet won't change either his clothes or his attitude.

Just after midnight one night, a guard named Francisco is walking on a platform in front of the castle so he will be in plain sight of any approaching enemy.

"Stand and unfold yourself," he cries out when a second guard, named Bernardo, approaches. Why Bernardo has folded is not explained, but the late hour might have something to do with it. Anyhow, Francisco has a right to be suspicious, for it turns out that Bernardo has come to relieve him of his watch.

Two other guards, Horatio and Marcellus, join the group, and their idle chatter turns to ghosts. Marcellus and Bernardo claim to have seen the ghost of the ex-King of Denmark, Hamlet's father, several nights running.* Horatio is a skeptic and won't be convinced until he sees the ghost with his own eyes.

The ghost promptly obliges, appearing in full armor, heavy though it is on his ectoplasm.

"Mark it, Horatio," whispers Bernardo, who has an orderly mind. But Horatio can't find a pencil, and isn't sure it would show on a ghost anyhow.

Horatio tries to engage the ex-King in conversation, but, never having passed the time of night with a ghost before, can think of nothing better than "Speak to me" (or, in some texts, "Spook to me"), which is a feeble opening gambit. Finally, after an awkward silence, the ghost hears a cock crow and clanks off. Horatio thinks that if anyone can get the ghost to talk it would be Hamlet, since blood is thicker than water.† So they go off to fetch him.

Before they leave, Horatio cries, "Break we our watch up." He is obviously distraught.‡

Hamlet, meanwhile, is in the castle, where the King and Queen are trying to cheer him up.

"How is it that the clouds still hang on you?" asks the King, who is interested in meteorological phenomena. But Hamlet is of no help, having majored in philosophy.

"Seek not for thy noble father in the dust," counsels the Queen, having noticed Hamlet poking around behind the furniture. But he goes on brooding, and running his finger along the tops of shelves.

---

* *And out of breath.*
† *And much thicker than whatever the ghost has in his veins.*
‡ *Or else time means nothing to him.*

After the King and Queen exeunt, which they do frequently, having been married only two months, Hamlet is left muttering to himself.

"O that this too too solid flesh would melt!" he groans. He has been dieting for weeks, trying to get into condition after going on a binge of Danish pastry.

The next night, having been told of the ghost by Horatio, Hamlet mounts the platform and takes his post, needing something to defend himself with. He is full of anticipation, never having seen the ghost of a close relative before, and somewhat uncertain about protocol. Promptly at midnight the ghost appears, his face looking so gray that Hamlet is about to ask him if he is ill, when he remembers. Taking Hamlet aside, he makes what is obviously a prepared speech.* The climax of it comes when he asks Hamlet to avenge his "foul and most unnatural murther."

* *The original ghost-written address.*

"Murther!"

"Murther?" Hamlet asks incredulously. He thinks the ghost must surely mean "mother," and this seems like strong language to use even about Gertrude.

"Murder," says the ghost, dropping the lisp, "murder most foul." He goes on to say that it was he, Hamlet's father, who was murdered, and by none other than Hamlet's uncle.

"Uncle!" cries Hamlet at this point, but the ghost won't be stopped, and continues to describe every gruesome little detail. It seems that he had been catching forty winks in the garden when the murderer crept up and poured poison in his ears.* This way the victim was unable to detect the telltale taste and spit it out. Nor, with his ears awash, could he hear the murderer's departing footsteps. It looked like the Perfect Crime.

Having told his story, the ghost turns on his heel to get back to Hell before they call the roll.

"Whither ghost?" asks Hamlet, but gets no reply.

It is almost daybreak, and it dawns on Hamlet. He swears to have revenge on King Claudius for the dastardly deed, and to make his mark.†

"O, fie!" he swears, looking around first to be sure no ladies are present. "O, fie!"

When Horatio and Marcellus run in, Hamlet makes them swear on their swords, which they find ridiculous and uncomfortable, never to blab about what they have witnessed this night.

"Swear," puts in the ghost, who is under the platform, burrowing for all he's worth but making slow headway toward Hell and still able to take part in the conversation.

---

* Actually "in the porches of my ears" is what the ghost says. His ears must have been pretty sizable, with steps and everything.
† On King Claudius.

Before they leave the platform, Hamlet, Horatio, and Marcellus argue about the hour and try to synchronize their watches. "The time is out of joint," says Hamlet in disgust.

Hamlet acts crazy

Now Hamlet knows his father has been murdered by his uncle, but he has only a ghost's word for it, and this is pretty flimsy evidence.* He decides to get some more proof, and meanwhile to pretend he is off his rocker so as to catch the King off his guard. As long as he appears insane, he can act with impunity, a poniard, or anything else that comes to hand. He has no fear of being committed, a little insanity being expected of members of the royal family, whose parents were usually first cousins.

The first person he tries this out on is Ophelia, his girl friend, a sensitive creature who comes unhinged easily. Upset on finding her fiancé gone berserk overnight, she runs to tell her father, Polonius, a garrulous old windbag who is adviser to the King and to anyone else who will listen.

Bursting into Polonius' room, Ophelia looks as if she has seen a ghost. Actually she is one of the few who hasn't.

"How now, Ophelia, what's the matter?" asks Polonius. Her eyes are starting from their sockets and there's no telling where they will go if they aren't stopped. Polonius, an observant father, figures that something is amiss.

"My lord, as I was sewing in my closet," she begins, without explaining why she picked a place with such poor light, "Lord Hamlet, with his doublet all unbrac'd, no hat upon his head, his stockings fouled, ungarter'd, and down-gyved to his ankle, pale as his shirt, and his knees knocking each other, comes

* *It wouldn't stand up in court, and any judge could see through it.*

before me." At first she thought he was looking for the W.C. and had opened the wrong door. But when he grabbed her by the wrist and backed off at arm's length, she knew he was not his normal self. He had never backed off before.

Polonius sizes up the situation at once.* "This is the very ecstasy of love," he says firmly. He knows all the symptoms: the hatlessness, the hopelessness, and the walking knock-kneed to try to keep the stockings up. His daughter has driven the Prince mad with desire, and he is rather proud of her.

"Come, go we to the King. This must be known," he tells Ophelia, hustling her off to the castle. Polonius loves to be a bearer of tidings, whether good or bad.†

In the castle the King and Queen are talking with two courtiers named Rosencrantz and Guildenstern, who in any

---

* *He gets the wrong size, as usual.*

† *Had he been a woman, Polonius would have been known as a gossipmonger. But adviser to the King was the male equivalent.*

Not his normal self

R. and G.

other time would have been members of a comedy team or a law firm. The King, who hasn't yet heard Polonius' story, has noticed Hamlet acting strangely of late, and he asks R. and G., who have known him since boyhood, to do a little private detective work. When they agree, the King says, "Thanks, Rosencrantz and gentle Guildenstern," and the Queen says, "Thanks, Guildenstern and gentle Rosencrantz." Either they play no favorites or they can't tell the two men apart.

"I have found the very cause of Hamlet's lunacy," Polonius blurts out as he hurries up to the King.

"O, speak of that. That do I long to hear," begs the King, who loves nothing better than having someone talk to him about the mental aberrations of his kinfolk.*

* There is evidence that the King once considered a career in psychiatry, but gave it up when there was a sudden vacancy on the throne.

"Since brevity is the soul of wit," Polonius begins, "I will be brief." The speech that follows, however, is neither short nor funny. It includes reading the full text of a love letter from Hamlet to Ophelia in which Hamlet quotes a poem of his own composition which was apparently so statistical, perhaps enumerating Ophelia's charms, that it sickened even the author. ("I am ill at these numbers," is the way he puts it.) While Polonius is still talking, he sees Hamlet approaching and hustles the King and Queen out of the room.

"I'll board him," he says. Polonius board everybody.

Hamlet enters with his nose in a book.* Polonius, testing his sanity, asks him a searching question. "Do you know me, my lord?"

"Excellent well. You are a fishmonger," Hamlet answers, not even coming close.

As the questioning proceeds, Polonius becomes increasingly certain that Hamlet is out of his head because of unrequited love, which is one of the worst kinds. Actually, as we know, Hamlet is playing a part, which means that anyone who plays the part of Hamlet is really acting.

Rosencrantz and Guildenstern now come in to try to find out what is wrong with their old classmate. But Hamlet uses doubletalk, which they are unable to figure out even though there are two of them.

"I am but mad north-northwest," he says, peering at a compass and laughing eerily. "When the wind is southerly I know a hawk from a handsaw." † What he means is that he is only crazy when he wants to be, but R. and G. don't get it. They

---

* So as not to lose his place.

† "Handsaw" is probably a corruption of "hacksaw" or "Hawkshaw" or something. Corruption was rife in those days.

think Hamlet is addlepated and Hamlet thinks they have holes in their heads. He is nearer right than they are.

Hamlet is tested some more

Polonius still wants to prove to the King that Hamlet is mad about Ophelia. Yet busy as he is, barking up the wrong tree, he still has time to give advice. While his son, Laertes, is packing his bags to go to France, the helpful father stands by and hands him old saws.*

"Give every man thy ear, but few thy voice," he advises his son, knowing you can always get a hearing aid but vocal cords are irreplaceable. And "Neither a borrower nor a lender be," he counsels, hoping the lad will think twice before writing home for money.

Once Laertes is gone, Polonius goes back to minding

* See "handsaw," above.

Polonius advises his son

Hamlet's business. He suggests to the King that they hide behind the arras and eavesdrop on Ophelia and Hamlet. "I'll loose my daughter to him," says Polonius, who has kept her on a leash ever since she became interested in boys.

While the King and Polonius are hiding behind the arras, Ophelia, the bait, walks up and down reading a book, although her heart isn't in it.

Hamlet comes in, looking ghastly, all "sicklied o'er with the pale cast of thought," and muttering to himself loud enough for people in the second balcony to hear.*

"To be or not to be," Hamlet says profoundly, making a simple statement sound so philosophical that it has led to hundreds of scholarly interpretations. Then he talks about suffering from slingshots and arrows, taking his arms out of the sea, shuffling off a coil, and making his quietus (a small carved object) with a bodkin.† Since he doesn't know anyone is listening, and has no reason to pretend, maybe he really *is* crazy.

"Good my lord," Ophelia greets him pleasantly, "how does your honor for this many a day?" It's his mental health she is interested in, but she asks about his honor so as not to be too obvious.

"I humbly thank you, well, well, well," Hamlet replies, his tongue getting caught in his teeth toward the end.

Ophelia is sweet and gentle with Hamlet, offering to return his old love letters. But he denies ever having written them. Even if he had, what would he want with old letters anyhow, he snarls. He's not collecting stamps.

Finally Hamlet screams at her, "Get thee to a nunnery," and

* *The medical term for this sort of thing is a soliloquy.*
† *Whose bodkin? Od's?*

stomps out. Ophelia is left with her memories and a pile of old letters. She is too innocent to think of blackmail or breach of promise.

As the King and Polonius come from behind the arras, the King says this doesn't look like love to him—anyway, not as he remembers it. He's also beginning to think that Hamlet's pate isn't addled after all, and that he has something else on his mind. Maybe he could be sent on a business trip to England, where his madness wouldn't be so noticeable. Anyhow, the sea air might clear his head or at least unstop his nasal passages. Hamlet's heavy breathing is beginning to worry the King.*

The play within a play

Hamlet, for his part, isn't growing any fonder of his uncle. "Bloody, bawdy villain! Remorseless, treacherous, lecherous, kindless villain" is the best he can say for him.

"He breaks my pate across, plucks off my beard and blows it in my face, and tweaks me by the nose," Hamlet exaggerates, "and I just sit here and take it." He is beginning to think there is something wrong with him internally. "Methinks," he says clinically, "I am pigeon-livered."

An idea comes to him when he meets a troupe of actors who have just had a long run, although we are not told from where.† One of their plays, *Caviar to the General,* is about a high-ranking officer who was murdered with some tainted fish eggs. Hamlet decides to alter the script slightly to make it similar to the ghost's story, and then watch the King while the King watches the play.

But first Hamlet, who so far as we know has never done

---

* *It keeps the tapestries in a constant flutter.*
† *Probably from wherever they opened.*

any acting, gives the players detailed advice on how to play their parts. "Speak the speech trippingly," he tells them, rolling an "r" back and forth across his tongue. The actors listen respectfully, whatever they may think,* because Hamlet is paying the bills.

So the play is put on. Part of it is a dumb show, and the rest of it is not much cleverer. To help the King get the idea, the actors hold up a sign reading: "Any resemblance to persons living and dead is purely intentional."

When they get to the point where a murderer pours poison into the sleeper's ears, the King's gorge rises.†

"Give me some light," he shouts, as if unable to read his

* Some think he is gargling.
† The king rises with it.

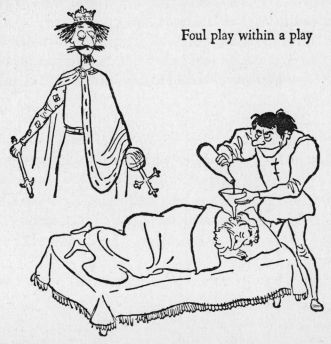

Foul play within a play

program. His face is deathly pale, and the curl has gone out of his beard. Exit the King, sickened.

"Ah, ha!" Hamlet cries, half exulting and half laughing. When Rosencrantz and Guildenstern bring him word that the King is suffering from a sore throat caused by his choler, Hamlet knows that the ghost spake the truth about his father's murder.

" 'Tis now the very witching time of night," he mutters to himself, feeling the devilish impulse to go out and ring doorbells. Then, seized by a sudden thirst for a warming drink, he adds, "Now could I drink hot blood!" *

Hamlet visits his mother

Elsewhere in the castle the King is pacing about, taking steps to get rid of Hamlet. Finally he decides to pray. It might do some good, and it can't hurt. Or so he thinks until he tries to kneel.

"Bow, stubborn knees," he says, so accustomed to giving orders that he dictates to his own joints.

Hamlet, who is down the corridor a few hundred yards, hears the creaking and comes over to see what's up and who's down. The King is so busy trying to remember a prayer, any old prayer, that he doesn't notice his nephew-stepson (and would-be murderer), who stands right behind him with a naked sword.

"Now might I do it Pat," Hamlet says to some Irishman not listed among the characters.

But Hamlet is a man who can't act.† Besides, his mood has

---

* But he had to go thirsty, all the blood banks being closed at that time of night.

† Unfortunately also true of many who play Hamlet.

Hamlet hesitates

changed, and at this moment a cup of hot blood would be positively nauseating.

"Up, sword," he says to his well-trained blade. If killed now while praying, the King might go to Heaven, where Hamlet thinks he would spoil the tone of the place. Hamlet will wait until he is drunk, swearing, committing incest, or busy with one of his other pursuits.

At this point Hamlet is summoned to his mother's dressing room for a dressing down. What he doesn't know, unless he expects it as a matter of course, is that Polonius is hiding behind the arras,* taking down every word.

"Hamlet, thou hast thy stepfather much offended," says the Queen, who is given to understatement.

* *There seems to be an arras in every room in the castle. A water-proofed one is used as a shower curtain.*

Thereupon Hamlet brings out two snapshots that he just happens to have with him, one of the Queen's first husband (in his pre-ghost days) and one of her second, the present King. "See what a grace was seated on this brow," he says admiringly of the first, "Hyperion's curls, the front of Jove himself,* and an eye like Mars." As for the second, "This one," he sniffs, "looks like a mildewed ear." Either Hamlet is prejudiced or King Claudius had better replace the Court Photographer.

As Hamlet waxes excited over the comparison and waves the pictures wildly, the Queen grows frightened.

"What wilt thou do? Thou wilt not murder me? Help, ho!"

"What ho?" asks Polonius from his hiding place. He is slightly hard of hearing.

"Was that a rat?" asks Hamlet, noticing the rather squeaky voice. Without waiting for an answer, he whips out his sword and stabs Polonius through the arras.

To make the scene more confusing, the ghost of Hamlet's father now glides onstage in his nightgown, unable to sleep because of all the din. He looks more ghostly than he did in his armor.

"Do not forget! This visitation is but to whet thy almost blunted purpose," the ghost tells Hamlet, making motions as if to sharpen something. "But look, amazement on thy mother sits.† Speak to her."

"How is it with you, lady?" asks Hamlet politely.

"How's it with you?" she replies.

Seeing that this sort of small talk isn't getting them any-

---

* *Whose rear, he doesn't say.*

† *Chairs seem to be at a premium in this scene. See above, " . . . grace was seated on this brow."*

where, Hamlet apologizes to the Queen for making a hole in the draperies and drags the body of Polonius into another room. For once, Polonius hasn't a thing to say.

Ophelia goes to pieces

When the Queen tells her husband of Hamlet's wild behavior, and how he mistook Polonius for a rat, the King is upset. "Where is he now?" he asks worriedly.

"Gone to draw apart the body he hath killed," replies the Queen, apparently thinking that Hamlet is now dismembering poor old Polonius.

The King shudders. "Ho, Guildenstern!" he shouts, and in come both Rosencrantz and Guildenstern. The same thing would have happened if he had shouted, "Ho, Rosencrantz!" He orders them to take Hamlet to England. They are also to take sealed instructions to the King of that country, indicating that Hamlet is expendable.*

Once Hamlet is on his way to England, the King breathes easier, and breathing has always been a matter of considerable importance to him.

But he and the Queen get a nasty jolt when Ophelia comes in, singing off-key and strewing † flowers all over the place. The death of her father and the madness of her lover have lowered her I.Q. to a point where it can no longer be measured. To make matters worse, Laertes has suddenly returned from France and makes a scene (Scene V) because his father was buried before he could get to the funeral. Here

---

* *In those days kings were always doing little things like this for each other.*

† *It is one of the oddities of the English language that everything else you throw, but flowers you strew.*

34

Enter Ophelia

they've spent all that money for mourners, when he would have done it for nothing.

Meanwhile Ophelia, not to be outdone, is singing "Hey non nonny, nonny, hey nonny," and other popular songs, and madly passing out flowers to everyone within reach. The King begins to wonder whether he has sent the right party to England.

"There's rosemary, that's for remembrance, and there's pansies, that's for thoughts," * she says as she hands a few blooms to Laertes, not realizing how embarrassed the poor lad is, standing there with a bouquet in his hands. Then she deals out fennel and columbines to the King and daisies and rue to the Queen. "And here's some for me," she says, not wanting to leave anybody out. The poor girl may be pretty far gone, but

* *She is completely wacky, and so is her grammar.*

she still knows her flowers. Even if she doesn't become Princess of Denmark, she would make a good Queen of the May.

The end of Ophelia *

Word comes to the King that Hamlet has got loose from Rosenstern and Guildencrantz and is headed home.

"To the quick of the ulcer," the King says crisply to Laertes, not wanting to beat around the abdomen. "What would you like to do to the fellow who has stabbed your father through the arras and driven your sister flower-strewing?"

"Cut his throat i' the church," snaps back Laertes, who visualizes the consternation of the preacher and the people in nearby pews.

"No," says the King soothingly. "There's a better way." Laertes has quite a reputation as a swordsman, and the King proposes that he engage Hamlet in a friendly bout in which Hamlet will be given a rapier with a blunt end, while Laertes will use a nice sharp blade with poison on the tip. In case anything goes wrong, they will offer Hamlet a poisoned drink to cool him off permanently. Laertes agrees, having nothing to lose but a few minutes of his time.

At this moment the Queen comes running in. She is upset by something, possibly Laertes' sword. "One woe doth tread upon another's heel," she says, as soon as she gets to her feet again. His sister, she tells Laertes, has gone to a watery grave, and must be moved to a cemetery on higher ground. It seems that Ophelia was hanging garlands on the limb of a willow tree, trying to improve on nature, when the limb broke and she fell into the brook. The Queen, a frustrated pulp writer, describes the scene vividly.

* *"There's a divinity that shapes our ends," said Hamlet once, in happier days, as he watched Ophelia walk gracefully away from him.*

"Her clothes spread wide, and, mermaid-like, awhile they bore her up, which time she chanted snatches of old tunes." But then, she adds sorrowfully, "Her garments, heavy with their drinks,* pulled the poor wretch from her melodious lay to muddy death." Why the person who gave the Queen this detailed account didn't fish Ophelia out is not explained. Perhaps he knew the plot.

"Alas, then, she is drowned," exclaims Laertes, hazarding a guess.

"Drowned, drowned," the Queen says, sure enough of the result of long immersion to speak firmly and repetitiously.

"Too much of water hast thou, poor Ophelia, and therefore I forbid my tears," says Laertes, fearful of making things any soggier.

𝔄 grabe situation

The last acts opens in a churchyard, where two jolly gravediggers are digging for comic relief. From time to time they lean on their spades and exchange witticisms. They seem to have grown calloused, especially on the palms. One gravedigger leaves for town to fetch a stoup of liquor, while the other, who feels sick to his stomach, sings dolefully as he digs, and now and then throws up a skull.†

Hamlet and Horatio enter the churchyard, and Hamlet exchanges pleasantries with the gravedigger, asking him, for instance, "How long will a man lie i' the earth ere he rot?" ‡ One of the skulls Hamlet has been fiddling with turns out to have belonged to Yorick, the court jester, who used to let

---

* *They had obviously had one too many.*
† *An early instance of skulldiggery.*
‡ *The gravedigger's answer, in case you, too, have been wondering, is about eight or nine years.*

Comic relief:
two jolly gravediggers

Hamlet ride on his back. Hamlet was attached to the fellow, and as he fondles the skull he grows nostalgic.

"Alas, poor Yorick," he sighs. The years have not been kind to his old friend.

Enters now a funeral procession, consisting of the King, Queen, Laertes, Mourners, and Ophelia. Everyone, except of course Ophelia, walks slowly, with downcast eyes. Hamlet and Horatio bend over a tombstone, pretending to be epitaph collectors. When the name of Ophelia is mentioned, Hamlet pricks up his ears.

"Lay her i' the earth," cries Laertes,* "and from her fair and unpolluted flesh may violets spring!" It seems appropriate that his sister should wind up as a flower bed.

Then, when Ophelia has been lowered into the grave, he jumps in with her and begs them to bury him too. "We are in this thing together," he says.

* *Dropping his n's, as usual.*

38

Thereupon Hamlet, not to be outburied, jumps in also. "This is I, Hamlet the Dane!" he cries, so they will carve his name correctly on the headstone.

Laertes, angered at thus being upstaged—whose sister's funeral is this, anyway?—grapples with Hamlet. They fight at close quarters, there not being room for anything else.

"I prithee," gasps Hamlet, always polite, "take thy fingers from my throat."

"Pluck them asunder," orders the King, realizing that without poisoned daggers, et cetera, the wrong man might get killed. At last he convinces the two hotheads that they should get out of the hole they are in and fight a proper duel where the spectators will have a better view.

None of this has been helping Ophelia any.

The duel

All the members of the court assemble to see the bout. It seems an uneven match, since Laertes is Champion of France and Hamlet isn't even ranked. What the odds-makers don't know is that Hamlet has been practicing for months, just on the chance of such an emergency. He is always expecting trouble, and isn't called the Melancholy Dane for nothing.

"There is special providence in the fall of a sparrow," says Hamlet apropos of nothing. And then, to prove he is good at wordplay, if not swordplay, he rattles off, "If it be now, 'tis not to come; if it be not to come, it will be now; if it be not now, yet it will come." When he concludes, the courtiers applaud enthusiastically. As an encore he runs through "Peter Piper picked a peck of pickled peppers."

At first Hamlet gets the better of Laertes, once touching him on the button * with his rapier, whereupon trumpets blare and symbols clash.† The King begins to stir restlessly.‡ He offers Hamlet a drink, but Hamlet says he wants to finish the duel first. The King makes it sound so refreshing, however, that the Queen takes a hearty gulp herself, and immediately swounds. She isn't heard from again.

About the same time, Laertes sticks Hamlet with his poisoned blade. Then, in a clumsy bit of swordplay, the rapiers get switched and Laertes himself is inoculated.

"They bleed on both sides," comments Horatio, who is sitting up close and can check both the left side and the right.

Laertes, stretched out on the floor, has a sudden change of heart. "Hamlet," he cries, "thou art slain." This is a surprise to Hamlet, who is the one still on his feet. Laertes also tells him that the King is behind everything. Actually the King is only behind the throne, cowering, and Hamlet, stung at last to action, runs him through with the very weapon that the King himself has poisoned. It is ironical, and very sharp.

Hamlet is now aware of everything except that he is still alive. "I am dead, Horatio," he says sadly. And then, when Horatio is not convinced, he reverses the word order: "Horatio, I am dead."

After two more speeches, he has nothing further to say on the subject, and Horatio whispers, "Good night, sweet Prince," apparently thinking he has dozed off.

As a matter of fact, Hamlet is a gone goose, along with the King, the Queen, and Laertes. The place is a mess, with

---

* Whether belly or collar is never made clear.

† Ever since, clashing symbols have been the curse of English literature.

‡ He wants to make sure the poison doesn't settle.

Hamlet, irritated

bodies, rapiers, and empty cups everywhere. It is fortunate that at this moment Fortinbras, a Norwegian prince who is next in line for the throne now that they have run out of Danes, arrives on the scene to clear away the debris. The Court Undertaker couldn't have coped with so much business all at once.

Fortinbras orders a cannon shot off, aimed, it is hoped, over the heads of the audience. A final fanfare is sounded, and the play ends on a tragic note, usually ascribed to one of the trumpeters.

1. Have you noticed how, in Shakespeare's plays, when people said they saw a ghost they usually did? Were people more trustworthy in those days? Were ghosts?

2. How long can you discuss Rosencrantz without mentioning Guildenstern, and vice versa?

3. What did Queen Gertrude see in King Claudius?

4. Where did Polonius spend his time when he was not skulking behind an arras?

5. Consider the effect on Ophelia's future if she had known how to swim.

6. Which is the most horrible line in the play? Not counting, of course, "O, horrible! O, horrible! Most horrible!" (I, v, 80)

7. Would it give you comic relief to hold in your hands the skull of an old friend?

8. Don't you think Hamlet had rotten luck? In fact was anything more rotten in the state of Denmark?

9. Deliberate on the King's request, "Come, Hamlet, come, and take this hand from me," followed by the stage direction: "The King puts Laertes' hand into Hamlet's." (V, ii, 213) Isn't this a little gruesome?

MACBETH

Introduction

As is frequently pointed out by the critics, Macbeth was probably written in haste. No one knows why Shakespeare was in a
hurry, unless he was nauseated by all the bloodshed. At any
rate this explains the unusually large number of tragic flaws
in the play.

It is the shortest of Shakespeare's major tragedies.* According to one theory, it was long in its original version and
subsequently cut. Most of the cutting was doubtless left in the
capable hands of Macbeth and the hired murderers, with Lady
Macbeth cheering them on.

Shakespeare, who never could think up a plot all by himself,
found this one in Holinshed's Chronicles, changing it just
enough so that no one would recognize the source.† If, as re-

* Some don't consider this a flaw.
† He didn't count on the resourcefulness of modern scholars, who
  have to discover things like this to become associate professors.

43

searchers say, Shakespeare took liberties with Scottish history, most of us who love liberty applaud him for it.

As Kittredge observes, Shakespeare at the beginning of the play "plunges, as usual, in medias res." Whatever this is, he doesn't come up for air until the play is over. Few Elizabethan dramatists had such powers of endurance as Shakespeare, and few modern theatergoers have such powers of endurance as the Elizabethans.

The play is full of atmosphere, which helps the characters breathe. Of the characters, the most interesting are Macbeth and Lady Macbeth. The latter is not only her husband's wife but his evil genius.* According to G. B. Harrison, "Lady Macbeth is at the same time greater and less than her husband,"

* All in all, quite a helpmate.

which is about as neat a trick as you will find in all Shakespeare. Cruel and heartless as they appear, both Macbeth and Lady Macbeth are said to have a gentle, loving side. It must be the side away from the audience.

There are some beautiful passages. One of them is the hallway in Macbeth's castle, where Lady Macbeth loved to fingerpaint on the wall with other people's blood.

Macbeth and the witches

Three witches, extremely weird sisters, are having a picnic amidst thunder and lightning somewhere in Scotland. Judging from their appearance, they placed one-two-three in the Edinburgh Ugly Contest.

"When shall we three meet again in thunder, lightning, or in rain?" asks one of them. They hate nice weather and are happiest when they are soaking wet and their hair is all stringy.

"When the hurly-burly's * done, when the battle's lost and won," another replies. A battle is going on between the forces of Duncan, the King of Scotland, and some Norwegians, assisted by the rebel Thane of Cawdor. At the moment it's looking good for Duncan, because two of his generals, Macbeth and Banquo, have cunningly put bagpipes into the hands of the enemy, who are blowing their brains out.

The witches hear some dear friends † calling, and depart. "Fair is foul, and foul is fair," they comment philosophically as they leave. This must have been pretty upsetting to any moralists, semanticists, or baseball umpires who chanced to overhear them.

Shortly afterward, the battle having been won by Macbeth,

* See also hurdy-gurdy, hunky-dory, and okey-dokey.
† A cat and a toad. Witches have to make friendships where they can.

and the weather having turned bad enough to be pleasant, the witches meet again.

"Where hast thou been, Sister?" asks one.

"Killing swine," the second replies. All three of them have been busy doing similarly diverting things, and one of them happily shows the others the thumb of a drowned sailor which she is adding to her thumb collection.*

Macbeth and Banquo come by at this point, on their way to inform the King that they have defeated the rebels. They would rather tell him in person than render a report in triplicate.

"Speak, if you can," says Macbeth boldly to the hags. "What are you?" He rather thinks they are witches, but would like to hear it from their own skinny lips.

* *In a comedy, this would be considered tragic relief.*

The witches start hailing

The witches start hailing.* They hail Macbeth as Thane of Glamis and Thane of Cawdor and say he will be King Hereafter. Not to leave Banquo out, they hail him as "lesser than Macbeth, and greater." (The witches are masters of gobbledyspook.) He won't be a king, they say, but he'll beget kings, and now they have to begetting along.

Macbeth knows he is Thane of Glamis, but has no idea (or didn't have until now) of becoming Thane of Cawdor or King Hereafter. "Stay, you imperfect speakers, tell me more," he commands. But the witches, perhaps not liking the way he refers to their elocution, vanish into thin air, making it slightly thicker.

While Macbeth is meditating about what the witches have forecast for him, a couple of the King's henchmen, straight from a busy day of henching, ride up. They bring word that Duncan is liquidating the Thane of Cawdor and giving his title to Macbeth, it being an inexpensive gift. (Duncan, as King of Scotland, was Scotcher than anybody.)

"Look how our partner's rapt," remarks Banquo, noticing that Macbeth, stunned with all the good news, acts as if he has been struck on the noggin. But Macbeth is only lost in thought, and will find his way out presently. Thus far the witches have been batting 1.000, and Macbeth is beginning to take more than a casual interest in Duncan's health.†

Duncan is done in

Back at Macbeth's castle, Lady Macbeth receives a letter in which her husband tells about the witches and how prophetic

---

* *Until now it has been raining.*
† *Henceforth when he says "How are you?" to the King it will be a bona fide question.*

their prophecies are proving. However, Lady Macbeth knows that her husband is a Weak Character. He would like to be king, but is embarrassed by any social unpleasantness, such as murdering a friend. Sometimes Lady Macbeth thinks there's something wrong with his circulatory system.

"It is too full o' the milk of human kindness," she mutters, remembering how easily his blood curdles. As for herself, she would ask nothing better than to be filled "from the crown to the toe, top-full of direst cruelty." She already has a good deal of the stuff in her, but thinks there is room for more.

Word comes that Duncan, on his way home from the battle and wanting to save the price of a hotel room, plans to spend the night with the Macbeths. Lady Macbeth rubs her hands with Glee, a Scottish detergent of those days, and prepares to entertain the royal guest. She seems to hear a raven croaking, and that's a sure sign of death.*

"Come, you spirits that tend on mortal thoughts," she cries out to whatever unseen spirits may be lurking in the murk, "unsex me here. Come to my woman's breasts and take my milk for gall." It is to the credit of the spirits that they do not accept her invitation.

By the time Macbeth arrives, Lady Macbeth has it all figured out. She tells her husband that they will wait until Duncan has gone to bed, ply his guards with drink, and then stab Duncan to death with the guards' daggers, thus not bloodying any of their own utensils.

Knowing that he shows everything on his face, including what he has eaten for breakfast, Lady Macbeth instructs her husband how to act. "Look like th' innocent flower," she says craftily, "but be the serpent under 't." Her last words are spoken with a menacing hiss.

* *At least of the raven.*

Macbeth at first has misgivings, wondering whether this is quite the sort of thing for him to do as Duncan's host. Also he is scared, but not as scared as he is of Lady Macbeth.

"If it were done when 'tis done, then 'twere well it were done quickly," Macbeth rattles off to his wife, hoping to confuse her.

"Screw your courage to the sticking-place," Lady Macbeth tells him, handing him his tool box. Macbeth finally agrees to go along, but he doesn't sound any too enthusiastic.

That night Macbeth finds himself on his way to the guest room, about to dispatch Duncan. Lady Macbeth has given the guards a Mickey MacFinn and taken their weapons, which she thoughtfully lays out for her partner in crime.*

"Is this a dagger which I see before me, the handle toward

---

* She thought at first of murdering Duncan herself. But as he lay sleeping, his mouth wide open and his teeth in the glass on the chair, he looked too much like her dear old father.

Macbeth has misgivings

my hand?" Macbeth asks himself. (It is.) He hears a wolf howl, starts, and keeps going.

In a few moments an owl begins hooting, crickets cry,* and bells ring. Duncan, whom Macbeth has stabbed, is the only one who keeps still. Then Macbeth imagines he hears someone cry out, "Macbeth does murder sleep—the innocent sleep, sleep that knits up the raveled sleave † of care." This has become an FSQ ‡ although carpers contend that it is nothing but a Mixed Metaphor.

Anyhow, he is too upset to put the bloody daggers by the guards, and Lady Macbeth takes over from her lily-livered husband.

"Infirm of purpose!" she addresses him tenderly, using a nickname she employs only when the two are alone together. "Give me the daggers." She carries them off, plants them by the guards, and is back in an instant, bloody but unbowed.

"I dare do all that may become a man," Macbeth says to her plaintively; "who dares do more is none." What he means is that it takes a woman to tackle the really dirty jobs.

Just then a knocking is heard. At first Lady Macbeth thinks it's her husband's knees, but then she realizes the doorbell isn't working and somebody wants in.

"Retire we to our chamber," she whispers to Macbeth, who is staring at his hands as if he has never seen them before.** Her idea is not to come out of retirement until they have removed all the telltale blood and climbed into their nighties. They exeunt.

---

* *Usually they chirp, but not in a situation like this.*
† *"Sleave," the scholars insist, is not the same as "sleeve," but no one is convinced.*
‡ *Famous Shakespearean Quotation.*
** *"What hands are here?" he asks.*

The knocking continues, and a porter goes to the gate. He takes his time,* being busy speculating about Hell. (Shakespeare's porters are invariably Philosophers.) "Anon, anon," he calls to the persons outside, not knowing their names.

The knockers, who are really boosters, are two of Duncan's henchmen—Macduff (in some texts Macduffel) and Lennox. They ask for Macbeth, and when he comes in, pretending to have been awakened by the uproar, they inquire about Duncan.

"Is he stirring?" asks Macduff.

"Not yet," Macbeth replies, having a hard time keeping a straight face. " 'Twas a rough night," he adds, trying to explain his rather rumpled appearance.

Macduff goes into Duncan's room, and shortly thereafter dashes out looking as if he has seen a corpse.

"O horror, horror, horror!" he screams. As soon as he can think of another word, he cries, "Awake, awake!" Quickly he turns the place into bedlam. "Ring the bell! Come, look on death itself!" People begin to queue up. When Lady Macbeth enters and is told that Duncan is murdered, her reaction is studied.† "What, in our house?" she says, simulating horror at the choice of locale. "Help me hence, ho," she cries, confident that some courteous courtier will offer his arm. But too much else of interest is going on. Not until she swoons and lies stretched out on the floor does anyone pay her heed ‡ and carry her out.

Naturally enough, the finger of suspicion points at the two guards, and Macbeth promptly kills them both before it swings around his way. Malcolm and Donalbain, Duncan's sons,

---

* He is a porter, isn't he?

† Especially by young tragic actresses.

‡ A small sum, or carrying charge.

"Oh horror, horror, horror!"

don't like the look of things and light out for England and Ireland, respectively, before somebody puts the finger on *them*.

So Macbeth ascends the throne, and Lady Macbeth is terribly proud of her husband and the way he is going up in the world.

𝕿𝖍𝖊 𝖌𝖍𝖔𝖘𝖙𝖑𝖞 𝖌𝖚𝖊𝖘𝖙

Macbeth should be happy as a king, but Banquo and his son Fleance disturb him. He remembers the witches' prophecy that Banquo is going to beget kings, and doesn't like the idea of having gone to all this trouble just to set up the throne for someone else's brats. Macbeth himself is the end of his line, and, although he doesn't know it yet, near the end of his rope.

Besides, he suspects Banquo of suspecting him of foul play.*

So he invites Banquo to dine one evening at the castle. While Banquo and Fleance are out on a horseback ride, getting up an appetite,† Macbeth calls in a couple of professional and fully licensed murderers.‡ Any more murders on his own, he fears, will lose him his amateur standing. The murderers, who are described as "without," though we never know what it is they lack, are quickly employed to practice their trade on Banquo and Fleance. They are despicable, heartless characters, and Macbeth is delighted to have made their acquaintance. "Your spirits shine through you," he says to them, trying to be complimentary but not knowing quite how to put it. Then he waves them on their way and bids them Godspeed, although it seems a little inappropriate.

Banquo and Fleance are riding around and around in the park, still feeling none too hungry. The murderers wait until their victims have dismounted,** and then set upon Banquo and stab him fatally. Before he dies, however, he warns Fleance.

"Fly, good Fleance, fly, fly, fly!"

Obediently, Fleance takes off. Although he gains elevation only by leaps and bounds, he is soon out of sight. The murderers have accomplished only half the job, but for once it was the little one that got away.

* *By coincidence, "Foul play" is precisely what a contemporary reviewer, writing in the* London Tymes, *said of* Macbeth.

† *Banquo has eaten at the castle before, and sitting at the same table with Lady Macbeth dries up his gastric juices.*

‡ *Later joined by a third, thought by some scholars to be Macbath in disguise, but more likely an apprentice murderer, getting experience.*

** *Shakespeare was part owner of the theater, and well aware that the cleanup crew charged extra if a horse was brought onstage.*

That night, at the banquet, Macbeth is just sitting down *
when one of the murderers sticks his bloodstained face in, explaining that he cut himself while shaving. He reports to Macbeth that Banquo is done for, with twenty gashes in his head. But while they were counting the gashes, Fleance escaped, and they'll settle for fifty cents on the dollar.

Macbeth goes back to the table, intending to enjoy his mead and potatoes, but when he gets to his chair he sees the ghost of Banquo sitting in it. He is disconcerted, to say the least.

"See! Behold! Look! Lo!" he cries,† but no one knows what's troubling him. They think he must be seeing things, which he is. Finally the ghost leaves, and Macbeth sits down,

* *"You know your own degrees," he says to his guests, all of them college men.*
† *A speech rich in ideas for the publishers of American picture magazines.*

The ghost of Banquo

56

mopping his brow with a slab of roast beef. Lady Macbeth tries to calm everyone.

"My lord is often thus," she says soothingly, but creating an unfortunate picture of their home life. "The fit is momentary." Then she whispers into his ear, "Take care, my lord, thou 'rt about to spill the beans."

Macbeth is just beginning to relax and regain his color, when Banquo's ghost reenters.

"Avaunt, and quit my sight!" Macbeth screams. The ghost avaunts, but not before some of the guests.* Lady Macbeth suddenly yearns to be alone with her husband.

"Stand not upon the order of your going," she hints to those who are still gossiping in the doorway, giving them a slight push and turning off the porch light.

Alone, Macbeth and Lady Macbeth look at each other disconsolately. It will be hard to win back their reputation for gay dinner parties. The evening is ruined, and there is nothing left to do but go to bed and have a few nightmares.

The witches again

Macbeth is in deep now, and knows it. It was all caused by the rosy picture, now turned blood-red, painted by the witches. Maybe, thinks Macbeth, he can ask the weird sisters a few more questions and find out what's going to happen in the fifth act.

Alone he strides the heath and, sure enough, comes upon the witches. These beauties are standing around a boiling caldron, fixing supper.

"Double, double toil and trouble," they moan as they stir

* *Macbeth is acting so insanely that he resembles Hamlet, and they fear they have stumbled into the wrong play.*

Fixing supper

the bubbling brew. Apparently they dislike cooking. As they stir, they toss in such ingredients as newts' eyes, goats' gall, poisoned entrails, bats' wool, lizards' legs, dragons' scales, and now and then the finger of a birth-strangled babe or a dash of baboon's blood for seasoning. They take care to follow the recipe * exactly, and, not surprisingly, seem in no rush to eat.

As Macbeth walks up, he hails them cheerily. "How now, you secret, black, and midnight hags!" He wants to ingratiate himself so they will answer his questions.

He seems to have said just the right thing, for they give him all sorts of interesting information. They advise him to look out for Macduff but otherwise not to worry, since (1) nobody born of woman shall harm him and (2) he won't be defeated

* *You can find this dish in Greta Ghoul's "Recipes for Retching" or in almost any diet cookbook.*

until Birnam Wood comes to Dunsinane Hill. From this he gathers that he is an excellent insurance risk.

The only thing that disturbs Macbeth is a little pantomime staged by the witches shortly before they vanish. In it, Banquo's ghost points to a long row of kings, and grins sickeningly. Since the ghost may have been sampling the witches' bat and lizard stew, this is understandable. Macbeth correctly interprets the show to mean that Banquo has outfoxed and outbegot him. However, he still doesn't see how he can be defeated by the present generation. Though no student of obstetrics, he is afraid of no man not born of woman, and it is his considered opinion that Birnam Wood will stay put.

"Who can bid the tree unfix his earth-bound root?" he asks of no one in particular, and receives no answer.

Macbeth gets his

Although unable to get at Macduff, who is vacationing in England, Macbeth hires some murderers to slay Macduff's wife and son.* Fortunately most of this domestic slaughter takes place offstage.

When Macduff learns that his family has been wiped out, he is sore annoyed, which is an ugly combination. Teaming up with Duncan's son, Malcolm, he raises an army. This takes time—you know how long it takes to raise a family.

"Front to front bring thou this fiend of Scotland and myself," he implores MacJove and the other Scottish gods, shuddering to think of Macbeth creeping up on him from behind.

Meanwhile Lady Macbeth, who has been trying to remove Duncan's blood from her hands for weeks, keeps washing

* The ready availability of murderers is a boon to Macbeth and to the plot.

"Out, damnèd spot!"

them without any luck.* When she isn't washing them, she is wringing them.†

"Out, damned spot!" she shrieks, losing her temper and foolishly thinking an imprecation will succeed where cleaning fluid has failed. Self-possessed as she was in the first act, she is now a bundle of nerves, and none too securely tied together.

Night after night she walks in her sleep, muttering about blood and Banquo's ghost. Unfortunately the Court Doctor hasn't even a love seat, much less a couch, in his office. He is

---

* See Glee, above.

† Sometimes she sniffs them. "All the perfumes of Arabia will not sweeten this little hand," she says sourly.

therefore "unable to minister to a mind diseased," and stands helplessly by.

"What's done cannot be undone," Lady Macbeth mutters, struggling with a knot in her stomach. As she sleepwalks, she carries a candle in her hand, leaving a trail of tallow drippings.* Finally she dies, this being the only way she can give up the ghost.

Macduff, Malcolm, and their army are now at Birnam Wood, while Macbeth remains at his castle at Dunsinane. "Tomorrow, and tomorrow, and tomorrow," he says over and over and over to himself, rather liking the sound.

Alarum clocks commence to go off, signaling the beginning of the battle. Macbeth rushes to the field, still thinking he leads a charmed life. Only when the enemy soldiers camouflage themselves with trees from Birnam Wood and start branching out toward Dunsinane does Macbeth realize that

* *"Out, brief candle!" commands Macbeth, addressing an inanimate object (as do so many of Shakespeare's characters) in the full knowledge that it can't talk back.*

Camouflaged as trees

the witches have played False with him. Then, when he gets into hand-to-hand, toe-to-toe conflict with Macduff, and Macduff casually mentions that he wasn't born of woman, or at least not in the usual way—he was "from his mother's womb untimely ripp'd" by some impatient obstetrician—Macbeth is ready to quit.

"Lay off, Macduff, I've had enuff" * is his unforgettable cry. But Macduff, warming to his task and sensing the final curtain, taunts his opponent.

"Yield thee, coward," he suggests, forgetting that Shakespearean heroes go down swinging.

Indeed, Macbeth has taken about all the guff from Macduff he can stand. "Lay *on*," he snarls, in a memorable change of prepositions.

The fighting is terrible, and it is fortunate for the audience that, like the slaughter of Lady Macduff and her son, it is off-stage. They thrust, parry, and lunge as if their lives depend on it. At last Macbeth begins to tire. He is bored † by Macduff, who also cuts off his head. This he gives to Malcolm, who is now King of Scotland and likely to get all sorts of unusual presents.

As the curtain is rung down, Malcolm invites everyone to come and see him crowned at Scone. The invitation does not apply to members of the audience, who at this point are too exhausted, anyhow, for further festivities.

* *Another version, no less authentic, is: "Lay ough, Macdough, I've had enough."*
† *Through the heart.*

𝕼uestions on 𝕸acbeth

1. Have you a weird sister? An odd brother?

2. Comment on the following quotation: " 'Aroint thee, witch!' the rump-fed ronyon cries." Discuss the advantages of rump-fed over spoon-fed and intravenous.

3. Was Macbeth thane? How does he compare in this respect with Hamlet?

4. Would you trust Lady Macbeth as a wet nurse? Keep in mind her expression of solicitude for her own infant: "I would, while it was smiling in my face, have pluck'd my nipple from his boneless gums and dash'd the brains out."

5. Which would you prefer in your stew:

    a. Newts' eyes?
    b. Dragons' scales?
    c. A dash of baboon blood?

6. Continue and bring to an interesting conclusion Lady Macbeth's unfinished poem:

> "The thane of Fife
> Had a wife. . . ."

7. If you have trouble remembering lines, take the part of one of the witches in the following scene:

1ST WITCH. Hail!
2ND WITCH. Hail!
3RD WITCH. Hail!

8. "Upon my head," said Macbeth, "they placed a fruitless crown." What did he expect, a bowl of grapes and bananas?

9. Did you realize that a hautboy is not a male child but a musical instrument?

10. Try to piece together the history of Scotland. Use Scotch Tape if necessary.

A MIDSUMMER
NIGHT'S DREAM

Introduction

A Midsummer Night's Dream *is often selected for study in school because, although it is about love, it is such a clean play. The reason for this may be, as one critic has said, that it is* "bathed in a flood of exquisite lyric verse." * *Moreover, though its heroes and heroines sleep side by side in the woods, they are not only innocent but too tired and confused to take advantage of the situation. As one of the most complicated plays Shakespeare ever wrote, it gives the teacher a sense of superiority to straighten it out in front of spellbound students.*

The date of A Midsummer Night's Dream is uncertain, but scholars assure us that it could not have been written as early as 1565, when Shakespeare was only one year old and pre-occupied with learning to write simple sonnets. Nor could it have been written as late as 1618, when he had been buried for two years and his inspiration probably had dried up. What-

* "Liquid verse" *is the term used by the same writer elsewhere, while commenting on the watered-down style.*

ever the precise date, internal evidence, notably some bits of tobacco discovered between the pages of the First Quarto, indicates that Sir Walter Raleigh had already returned from the Virginia Colony.

Quite obviously A Midsummer Night's Dream was written for the court, where people could be ordered to attend. It is possible that the play was meant to compliment Queen Elizabeth, who could identify herself with either Titania, the Queen of the Fairies, or Hippolyta, the Queen of the Amazons, depending on whether she felt dainty or muscular at the moment. There may even have been a veiled hint that Elizabeth, the Virgin Queen, could make good use of a love potion.

The plot is interwoven of several threads. These were taken from Chaucer, Plutarch, Ovid, and an outgrown doublet that Shakespeare inherited from Edmund Spenser. The story of the fairies is old hat, borrowed from the Earl of Derby. The central theme, it is often pointed out, is "the irrational nature of love," but let us not overlook the possibility of the irrational nature of Shakespeare.*

One question, never satisfactorily answered by scholars, is this: did Shakespeare's A Midsummer Night's Dream *result from something he ate?*

* And what, the reader may ask, of the characters? If they seem a bit wooden, it may be that Shakespeare wished them to feel at home in the forest, where most of the action takes place.

Theseus lays down the law

The scene of the play is Athens and Environs, two cities in ancient Greece. Theseus, the Duke of Athens, has won Hippolyta, Queen of the Amazons, with his sword. They met on the battlefield, and it was love at first sight when they glimpsed each other's bulging biceps. He asked her to be his and pressed his sword against her throat.* She swallowed hard and as-

* Tenderly, not wanting to cause any unsightly scars.

He asked her to be his

sented. As the play opens, it's only four days until their wedding, and Theseus keeps looking at his watch.

"Now, fair Hippolyta, our nuptial hour draws on apace," says Theseus happily. He is lolling on the royal sofa, idly watching his bride-to-be work out with bar bells.

In accordance with the custom of the day, Theseus is planning some entertainment for his wedding night, although this seems somewhat unimaginative. At any rate, he sends Philostrate, his Master of the Revels, to fetch some revelry, and maybe a little pomp and circumstance.

At this moment Egeus, an Athenian nobleman, rushes breathlessly into court,* followed by his daughter, Hermia (possibly a misprint for Hernia) and her suitors, Demetrius and Lysander.†

"Full of vexation come I," announces Egeus, who has a swollen look. What's troubling him is that Hermia wants to marry Lysander, while he insists that she marry Demetrius. Hermia, for obvious reasons, is under a strain.

"That man hath bewitched the bosom of my child," he declares, pointing an accusing finger ‡ at Lysander but not explaining the anatomical reference. Hermia's bosom looks perfectly all right.** "And furthermore," he charges, "he hath by moonlight at her window sung." Poor Egeus, remembering all that caterwauling, is too upset to care about word order.

Theseus, wishing to dispose of the case quickly so he can give his full attention to Hippo, rules that Hermia must either marry Demetrius, as her father desires, or spend her life in a nunnery, where there is small chance of her marrying any-

* *The Duke also seems to be a judge.*
† *It is impossible to tell Demetrius from Lysander. Don't bother to try.*
‡ *All his other fingers are noncommittal.*
** *Or at least she manages to put up a good front.*

70

body. With Theseus, everything is either black or white, which results, among other things, in his being bored by sunsets. He gives Hermia four days to decide, and sweeps out. The place needed it.

Away to the woods

Left alone, Hermia and Lysander bewail their fate. "Ay me! The course of true love never did run smooth," sighs Lysander, thereby slipping quietly into *Bartlett's Familiar Quotations*. Then an idea comes to him. He has an aunt who lives in a town some distance away, where the marriage laws are more lax than in Athens. The town isn't named, but it's probably somewhere in Nevada.

"Steal forth tomorrow night," he tells Hermia, "and in the wood there will I stay for thee." How he is going to get into the wood, he doesn't explain.*

While they are talking over their plans, Helena approaches.† She is the large, statuesque type who can see what is going on at a parade and is always looking for tall men. Demetrius is tall and Helena is mad for him. But Demetrius is mad for Hermia who is mad for Lysander—and there you have the situation (b.l.p) ‡ of *A Midsummer Night's Dream*.

"O, teach me how you sway the motions of Demetrius' heart," begs Helena, who would like to quicken his pulse just once.

"I frown upon him, yet he loves me still,"** replies Hermia, who is as baffled as anybody. She doesn't want any part of

---

* *Perhaps the explanation lies in the fact that he's a bore.*
† *She should have waited for them to get off the green.*
‡ *Before love potion.*
** *Though he loves her still, she usually runs as soon as he comes in sight.*

Demetrius, even the choicest. She cheers up Helena, however, by telling her that she and Lysander are meeting in the
woods the next night and going away from Athens forever.
This will leave the field (and the woods) clear for Helena.

"Until tomorrow night, then," says Lysander, waving
good-by with an embroidered handkerchief, "when Phoebe
doth behold her silver visage in the wat'ry glass, decking with
liquid pearl the bladed grass." He is given to ornate speech,
and as far as Helena is concerned, Hermia can have him.

"Farewell, sweet playfellow," says Hermia cheerily to
Helena, "and good luck with Demetrius."

Helena, elated, decides to tell Demetrius of the forthcoming
rendezvous in the woods, and then be on hand to catch him
on the rebound. The harder they fall, she theorizes, the higher
they bounce.

An odd lot of people * are assembled in Peter Quince's carpenter shop in another part of Athens. They are Quince, Nick Bottom (a weaver, especially when he is drunk), Francis Flute (a bellows-mender), Robert Starveling (a tailor), and Tom Snout (a tinker, though we are not told what he tinks about). Also in the company, naturally enough, is Snug, a joiner. If the names of these people seem rather peculiar, one must remember, as Shakespeare didn't, that they are Greeks.

These "rude mechanicals," as they are called, although they are no ruder than the others, are gathered to practice a play, *Pyramus and Thisby*, which they are going to put on for Theseus as part of his wedding night entertainment. Bottom

* *Such people seem to come in odd lots.*

An odd lot of Thespians

wants to play all the parts, and does a good deal of bellowing. (If this keeps up, the bellows-mender may come in handy.) Finally, everyone having been assigned his part, Quince tells them to be ready for a rehearsal in the woods the next night.

It's beginning to look as if we won't be able to see the woods for the people.

Enter the fairies

The next night, also in the woods, Puck (alias Robin Goodfellow) and a Fairy meet. Puck is a merry sprite with quite a reputation for what he considers screamingly funny pranks, like hiding in people's drinks to give them an extra kick, or

Puck meets a fairy

pretending to be a chair and upsetting the occupant. It's his job to keep Oberon, King of the Fairies, in stitches.

"How now, spirit," asks Puck, "whither wander you?"

"Over hill, over dale, through brush, through briar, over park, over pale, through flood, through fire," says the Fairy, obviously a letter carrier whom nothing stays from completion of his (or her) appointed rounds. At the moment, however, the Fairy is busy looking for dewdrops, hanging pearls in cowslips' ears, and doing other odd jobs you would have to be a fairy to appreciate.

Oberon, with his train, and Titania, the Fairy Queen, with her train, enter from opposite directions.* Oberon and Titania have been sleeping in separate acorn cups, because Titania has a young lad among her attendants whom Oberon wants her to give up. It may be that Oberon suspects he isn't really a fairy.

"Ill met by moonlight," says Oberon grumpily when he sees his wife. He enjoys his moonshine more when she isn't around.

They exchange some sharp words, Titania charging Oberon with having an affair with Hippolyta (which Oberon, in view of his size, is hardly up to), and Oberon insinuating that Titania has been dallying, and possibly dillying, with Theseus (who couldn't see her without a magnifying glass). Overcome by jealousy, they don't realize how small they are being.†

After Titania leaves with her train in a huff (and a chuff, chuff), Oberon plots to discomfit her, leaving her without a comfit to her name. He orders Puck, who can go anywhere in a trice,‡ to hustle off and fetch a certain flower, the juice of

---

* *The place is beginning to look like Grand Central Station.*

† *Because of a shortage of actors and actresses only a half-inch tall, the Fairies are usually played by ordinary-sized people.*

‡ *A Fairy tricycle.*

which, when rubbed on the eyelids of a sleeping person, will make him fall madly in love with the next creature he sees.* The trick, of course, is to rub the sleeper's eyelids without waking him.

"I'll put a girdle round about the earth in forty minutes," boasts Puck, zooming off with a corset in his hands.

Left to himself, Oberon chuckles about how he will use the juice of the flower on Titania when she is asleep, and how she will then fall in love with the first creature of the forest she sees on waking. Just then he hears someone coming.

"I am invisible," he says (else we might not have known), "and I will overhear their conference." There is no honor among fairies.

Demetrius comes running into the woods, with Helena hot on his heels. "Hence, get thee gone. I love thee not, therefore pursue me not," he says harshly. He is not one to beat around the bush, especially with a girl he doesn't care for.

"And even for that do I love you the more. I am your spaniel," says Helena, flapping her ears prettily.

"I'll run from thee and hide me in the brakes," threatens Demetrius. The brakes will stop her, he thinks to himself cunningly.

Oberon, who has been watching the whole thing, turns out to be a bit of a matchmaker, although among his tiny people he previously has had to match featherweights. He thinks it would be fun to turn the race around and have Demetrius chasing Helena. As soon as he gets that flower, he'll be rubbing it on many an eyelid.

* *What would happen if one eye were anointed and the other not, is thought-provoking.*

Oberon fires Titania

When Puck returns with the magic flower, Oberon takes it from him and, without so much as a thank-you, launches upon a famous speech.

"I know a bank where the wild thyme blows," he says, all the while running the flower through a juicer, "where oxlips and the nodding violet grows." There, he is certain, Titania will be found nodding with the violets. He gives Puck a little of the juice to fix up Demetrius, and he himself hies to the bank, where he believes Titania to be deposited.

When he arrives, Titania is getting ready for bed. "Sing me

77

now asleep," she commands, and the fairies sing a lullaby that knocks her out as effectively as a sleeping pill. While she is slumbering, Oberon sneaks in and drops some juice on her eyelids, hoping the first thing she sees when she wakes is something good and repulsive, like an ounce,* a pard, or a bore with rough whiskers.

Shortly afterward Quince, Bottom, and the rest of the mechanicals assemble in the woods to rehearse their play. Luckily for the plot, they pick a place close to where Titania lies sleeping, and Puck is watching them from behind some bushes.

"What hempen homespuns have we swaggering here, so near the cradle of the Queen?" Puck asks himself. Always up to some prank, he puts an ass's head on top of Bottom when he is offstage, and when the weaver comes in to recite his lines, the rest of the players flee in terror.

The first thing Titania sees when she awakens is Bottom. "What angel wakes me from my flowery bed?" she cries in ecstasy. "Come, sit thee down upon this bed, while I thy amiable cheeks do coy, and stick musk-roses in thy sleek smooth head, and kiss thy fair large ears." She can't seem to get over those ears of his—not without a ladder.

Bottom takes it all in stride, not being one to question his good fortune, even when Titania gives him four fairies named Peaseblossom, Cobweb, Moth, and Mustardseed.† They take care of his everyday wants, such as feeding him apricocks, fetching him jewels from the deep, and fanning moonbeams from his eyes. Bottom has never had such service before, even at the annual weavers' clambake.

* *A pound would be even better.*
† *These* could *be nicknames, let us hope.*

78

Bottom and Titania

"Let's have the tongs and the bones," * he suggests. And then, when thirst overtakes him, he calls for "a bottle of hay," perhaps planning to drink it through a straw.

Finally Bottom and Titania lie down on a bed of flowers, from which the thorns and thistles have been carefully removed. Bottom accepts everything nonchalantly, though he complains mildly that there are no sheets. "Sleep thou, and I will wind thee in my arms," says Titania soothingly.

While they sleep, Oberon, who is watching from a thicket, dances with wild Abandon † and laughs hysterically.

* *"Crude musical instruments," according to the authorities. Apparently the bones were picked up with the tongs, to avoid using one's fingers.*

† *A disreputable friend of his.*

In another part of the woods, Lysander and Hermia, who have lost their way, lie down to get some rest.

"One turf shall serve as pillow for us both," suggests Lysander, hoping to economize. But Hermia modestly insists that they leave a few feet of grass between them. It's a turf break for Lysander, but he takes it like a man.*

While they are sleeping, Puck happens by. He thinks Lysander must be the Athenian whom Oberon sent him after, and Hermia must be the poor girl who is chasing him fruitlessly. So he anoints Lysander's eyelids and is off.

As might be expected (by anyone who has read *The Comedy of Errors* or *The Two Gentlemen of Verona*), Helena, who is chasing Demetrius, stumbles on Lysander. The woods are full of reclining people, and she should have watched where she was going.

Awaking with damp eyelids, Lysander gropes about for his umbrella. He sees Helena, falls immediately in love, and starts

I.e., none too well.

Hermia chasing Lysander chasing → →

after her. "I would run through fire for thy sweet sake," he exclaims, knowing he is safe enough in these green woods.

No sooner have they gone than Hermia wakes up, notices Lysander isn't there, and tears off into the forest, fortunately in the right direction.

So now we have Demetrius being chased by Helena being chased by Lysander being chased by Hermia. Seldom have such a chased lot of young people been found in the woods anywhere. Puck has got things into a pretty mess with the juice of that little old flower. It's the sort of thing that should be sold only on prescription.

Everybody sleeps

Hermia, Lysander, Helena, and Demetrius get increasingly mixed up, as does the reader. Hermia and Helena, who in the first act were "two lovely berries moulded on one stem," have become detached, each with a stem of her own.

"Thou painted maypole," says Hermia, appraising the tall, symmetrical Helena.

→ → Helena chasing Demetrius

"You counterfeit, you puppet, you—" retorts Helena, trying to choose the exact word to describe her undersized rival.

"You dwarf, you bead, you acorn," adds Lysander helpfully.

However, Puck manages to avoid mayhem by leading everybody around the woods in a wild-goose chase. Thus no blood is shed, not even the goose's. He finally has all four lovers back where they started from and asleep on individual mossy beds.

"Lord, what fools these mortals be!" exclaims Puck as he looks at them lying there. He seems to forget that he was none too accurate with the love juice.

Oberon, thinking his little joke has gone far enough,* gets Puck to straighten out all the love affairs with another round of potion. "Crush this herb into Lysander's eye," he instructs him, losing patience and getting a little rough.

"Jack shall have his Jill," agrees Puck, who, understandably, has lost track of who's who by this time.

Insomnia seems to have been unknown in those days, or else it was all that chasing through the woods and the outdoor air † that did it. Anyhow, at this point in the play virtually everyone is asleep, and the reader may wish to take a little nap himself.

The awakening

Oberon begins to feel sorry for his fairy wife, Titania, and touches her eyes, meanwhile chanting, "Be thou as thou wast wont to be." She wonts to be awake, and very shortly is.

When she is shown the sleeping Bottom, of whom she has been so enamored, Titania is mortified. Even after his ass's head is removed, there is little improvement.

* The audience usually thinks so several scenes earlier.
† To say nothing of an occasional yawning chasm.

82

Little improvement

"Sound, music!" cries Oberon. "Come, my queen, take hands with me, and let's rock the ground." Then Oberon and Titania dance what is probably the first rock and roll, and afterward promise to be friends forevermore, even though married. As dawn is about to break, the fairies get the hell out of there. They know how silly they look in the daylight, and anyhow need to rest up for the next night's shenanigans.

Theseus, Hippo, and Egeus now arrive, dressed for the hunt.* "Good morrow, friends," Theseus politely greets the recumbent forms of Helena, Hermia, Lysander, Demetrius, and Bottom. When he gets no response, he leans over and yells into their ears, *"Good morrow, friends."*

"Bid the huntsmen wake them with their horns," Theseus

* *Fit to kill.*

commands, seeing the need for drastic measures. Thereupon several deep-chested men come in, place their trumpets, tubas, and other wind instruments against the sleepers' ears, and blast away. The lovers stir and ultimately awake, acting as if they have been drugged. They have.* All is soon explained, everything is forgiven, and it is evident that the play is really over. However, Quince and his friends have been rehearsing so hard in the forest that Shakespeare felt he owed them a performance. Hence the fifth act.

The wedding party

On the night of Theseus' wedding, all the lords and ladies are gathered to help him while away the hours until bedtime. Philostrate, the Master of the Revels, who hasn't been heard from since Act I, scene i, line 15, introduces Quince and his players, who are to put on *Pyramus and Thisby*. The audience expects the worst, and isn't disappointed.

In brief, which is the best way, the play is about two lovers who meet in a hole in the wall. Their love has not prospered, something having come between them.† So they plan a rendezvous in a jollier place, a tomb. Thisby gets there first, and is frightened off by a lion,‡ which pounces on her mantle and makes a bloody mess of it. After the lion leaves, Pyramus comes in, sees the bloody mantle, and, thinking Thisby dead, stabs himself repeatedly. (His dagger is the latest-model repeater.) Then Thisby returns, finds her lover dead, and stabs

* *We wish we could say, at this point, "Bottom's up." But he sleeps on through another sixty lines of exciting dialogue.*
† *The wall. See also* Romeo and Juliet. *Shakespeare loved walls.*
‡ *Those Greek zoo keepers were very careless.*

herself. Both of these young people play their parts up to the hilt.*

Theseus and the others laugh uproariously through the whole tragic performance. They take a superior attitude toward the actors, probably having seen the play at the Parthenon with the original cast. But it helps pass the time. Although it can have taken only a few minutes, Theseus says it is now midnight and time for bed.

The Duke and his party having gone bedward, Puck, Oberon, Titania, and the fairies take over and sing an itty-bitty ditty. They also try to dance, but trip the light fantastic and fall on their little faces. The last one left on the stage is Puck. He asks everyone who liked the show to applaud, and exits in a moment of absolute silence.

⚘ Questions on A Midsummer Night's Dream

1. *A Midsummer Night's Dream* has been called "Shakespeare's first undisputed masterpiece." Would you like to know by whom?
2. What is your idea of a wild thyme?
3. Bottom is said to have been "translated." What was his name in the original Greek?
4. Comment (ecstatically) on the poetic qualities of Puck's speech: "I go, I go; look how I go." Just how far gone was he?

---

* Come to think of it, the whole of Pyramus *and* Thisby *is a lot like* Romeo *and* Juliet. *Shakespeare was such a thoroughgoing plagiarist that he frequently stole from himself.*

5. Did you know that in Irish folklore Oberon is O'Brien?
6. Why do you suppose, with all the attractive Greek women around, Theseus married an Amazon? Could the best-looking Grecian ladies have been too busy posing for vases?
7. Do you think Bottom needed Puck's help to make an ass of himself?
8. What would you do if your mother had named you Pease-blossom, Cobweb, Moth, or Mustardseed? Would you, really?
9. Demetrius speaks of Helena's lips as "those kissing cherries." How fantastic can a lover get?
10. Suggest a more appropriate title for this play. For instance, *Much Ado about Nothing.* Or *All's Well That Ends.*

ROMEO AND JULIET

Introduction

The plot of Romeo and Juliet *came to England from Italy through France, arriving tired and dusty and covered with hotel stickers. Passed from person to person by word of mouth, it picked up interesting details and several of the more popular diseases of the sixteenth century. As with most of Shakespeare's works, scholars believe this also was preceded by a lost play. Elizabethans never could remember where they left things.*

Romeo and Juliet *is one of Shakespeare's early works. Microscopic examination of the First Quarto (Q1) reveals no trace of hair, and leads to the assumption that the play was written before Shakespeare grew a beard.* It unquestionably, perhaps even indubitably, belongs to that period of Shakespeare's life when he was experimenting with lyricism. The verse has a fluid quality, purple splotches being interspersed*

---

* *The First Quarto is known as a "bad" quarto, although we are not told what it did to get this reputation.*

with brown puddles where the author gave way to his weakness for liquid syllables.

The style in general is marked by numerous figures of speech—metaphors, semaphors, twongue-tisters, etc. An occasional wordy passage is offset by a passage of equal length in which Shakespeare strips his language bare and uses no words whatsoever. The stark simplicity of these latter passages beggars description.*

Shakespeare represents the love of Romeo and Juliet as that of two young people caught in the toils of Fate and unable to help themselves. In that hot Italian summer, passions were high and shirts were damp. Both of the lovers grow in stature as the story unfolds, until by the last act Romeo stands well over six feet in his sandals and Juliet has to let down the

* And, if long continued, might have impoverished the author.

hem of her kirtle. At the beginning of the play Romeo and Juliet are callow and impetuous; by the end of the play they are noble, dignified, and dead.

Romeo and Juliet *has long been one of the most popular of Shakespeare's plays, enjoyed especially by young people who identify themselves with the two lovers* * *and by poets who identify themselves with Shakespeare. The balcony scene has been played all over the world, except possibly in regions where there are only one-story houses. If the part of Juliet has sometimes overshadowed that of Romeo, it is because Romeo spends so much time under the balcony.*

* Young men tend to identify themselves with Romeo and young women with Juliet.

A family feud

The play opens with a Prologue which tells the whole story and makes it unnecessary to go any further.* It seems that in the Italian city of Verona a feud is going on between the Montagues and the Capulets, it being the height of the feudal period. What made the Montagues mad at the Capulets and vice versa is not explained. Evidently it's something that happened so long ago that nobody can remember, like Yale and Harvard. Anyhow, there's no feud like an old feud, and no one likes to upset a Tradition.

Since the Montagues and the Capulets carry swords and fight at the drop of a pizza, those red spots on the pavement really *are* blood. Hot-headed young fellows are always running swords through one another. "Draw!" they shout, which is the signal to pull their swords out of each other and look to see who made the larger hole.

Escalus, the Prince of Verona, is getting sick of all this bloodshed. Every time someone is killed, he loses a taxpayer.

"What, ho! you men, you beasts," he cries, making sure to include everyone. He warns Montague and Capulet that this

* *Anyone continuing is warned to look out for "the two hours' traffic of our stage," with dozens of Italians careening crazily to and from the wings.*

brawling has to stop, or they will forfeit their own lives. This puts a new complexion on things.*

"If there is any fighting from now on," Montague and Capulet promise, "it will be over our dead bodies." Escalus nods approvingly.

𝕽𝖔𝖒𝖊𝖔 𝖒𝖊𝖊𝖙𝖘 𝕵𝖚𝖑𝖎𝖊𝖙

Romeo, the son of Montague, is a handsome young fellow who is in an advanced stage of lovesickness for a girl named Rosaline. He sighs all day long, and is getting short of breath.†
At night he can hardly wait to get to sleep so he can start dreaming. But Rosaline cares for him not a whit.

Hoping to make him forget Rosaline, two swashbuckling friends of his, Benvolio and Mercutio, persuade him to crash

---

* *I.e., they turn pale.*
† *"Love is a smoke raised with the fume of sighs," he says, his head in the clouds.*

a party at the Capulets'. Since Romeo and Benvolio are Montagues, they don masks, hoping to be mistaken for burglars.

Old Capulet's daughter, Juliet, is the most luscious damsel at the party. When Romeo casts eyes on her, she playfully tosses them back. He feels an electric shock run through him, even though the place is lit by torches, and forgets Rosaline completely.*

"It seems she hangs upon the cheek of night like a rich jewel in an Ethiop's ear," remarks Romeo, who is a quick man with a simile, no matter how ridiculous. In a short while he has made her acquaintance, and before the evening is over has worked up to a kiss.†

"You kiss by the book," Juliet comments. Seems she has read the same how-to opus and recognizes the system. She puckers up again, ready to move on to the next chapter.

Tybalt, a young Capulet who hates the Montagues' guts, which he is always spilling into the gutter, recognizes Romeo by the way he smacks his lips.

"Fetch me my rapier, boy," he says to his caddy, passing up his broadsword and his eight iron. He is about to run Romeo through when he is stopped by old Capulet.

"Let him alone," Capulet says brusquely. Then, when Tybalt tries to argue, he shouts, "Go to!" Tybalt goes, although his destination is unspecified.‡

---

* *In fact the poor girl is never heard of again, thus missing her chance for immortality in what might have been Shakespeare's Romeo and Rosaline.*

† *He worked up from her neck to her lips, and hoped he hadn't gone too far.*

‡ *Shakespeare's two favorite devices for removing characters from the stage are "exeunts" and "go to's."*

"My rapier, boy," says Tybalt

At last Juliet's mother calls her, and Juliet withdraws.*
Later that night Romeo learns from Benvolio that Juliet is
a Capulet, and Juliet learns from her nanny that Romeo is a
Montague.

"I love a loathèd enemy," says Juliet, who is only fourteen
and a crazy, mixed-up Capulet.

As for Romeo, despite all that osculation he's none too sure
of himself. After all, Juliet has never seen him without his
mask on.

Romeo goes back for more

Later that night Romeo gives his friends the slip and climbs
over the wall into the Capulets' orchard. ("Leaps the wall,"
the text says, but Shakespeare was inclined to exaggerate.) He

* Her lips.

94

has a wonderful chance to purloin some fruit, but passes it up when he sees Juliet standing on her bedroom balcony in her negligee, looking negligected. At sight of her, Romeo goes slightly daft, mumbling about putting her eyes in the sky and replacing them with stars, probably two of the smaller ones.

"O that I were a glove * upon that hand, that I might touch that cheek!" he exclaims, getting more and more impractical.

Juliet, who has an extraordinary sense of smell, realizes that Romeo is in the vicinity. "O Romeo, Romeo!" (probably a misreading of "Aromeo, aromeo") she cries out. "Wherefore art thou at, Romeo?" And then, lest he take offense, she hastily adds, "A rose by any other name would smell as sweet."

As Romeo gazes hungrily at her, Juliet becomes embarrassed. "Thou know'st the mask of night is on my face," she explains, chagrined at being caught with her cold cream on. But in the pale moonlight, Romeo seems not to have noticed this.

They converse until almost morning, Juliet leaning from her balcony and Romeo pacing about underneath. At last she retires, chilled to the bone, and Romeo goes home with a crick in his neck.

Romeo and Juliet elope

Early the next morning Romeo calls on his friend, Friar Laurence, who is already up and puttering about in his garden, gathering a basketful of weeds for breakfast. "O, mickle is the powerful grace that lies in plants, herbs, stones," he mutters to himself as he works. Mickle, it appears, is a rare substance, rich in vitamins.

* *In view of Juliet's age, it would have to be a kid glove.*

"Good morrow, Father," Romeo greets him casually, as if he too were an early riser instead of one who hasn't been to bed. Forthwith he asks the priest to arrange a little marriage ceremony. When Friar Laurence learns that the bride-to-be is Juliet, he is delighted, it being something of a feather in his tonsure to marry a Montague and a Capulet.

At this point the plot is considerably helped by Juliet's nurse, a talkative old Cupidess who is always shuffling on and off stage, carrying notes. Apparently she is a practical nurse, with a special permit from the Postal Department.

Thanks to her efforts, Juliet meets Romeo at Friar Laurence's cell and they become mates.* Getting married in those days was simple. There were no questionnaires, no blood tests, no fingerprints. Moreover, a minor like Juliet didn't have to get her parents' consent, which was a good thing in this instance.

Juliet, now Mrs. R. Montague, goes back to her balcony. The nurse smuggles in a rope ladder which will be dropped that night as soon as Romeo arrives with a new soliloquy. It's not the most auspicious beginning for a marriage, but Romeo will soon be learning the ropes.

Some unfortunate swordplay

Tybalt, a hot-headed Capulet, is spoiling for a fight. It's a warm day, and, with no refrigeration, nothing keeps very well. Meeting Benvolio and Mercutio in the public square, Tybalt stands fast † and exchanges insults with them, at the current rate. But he is really much more interested in insulting Romeo, who at this moment arrives.

* *Cellmates.*
† *This is done by marking time at the double.*

"Thou art a villain," Tybalt snarls unsmilingly. This is pretty strong language, and Romeo should take umbrage.* But, remembering that he is now related to Tybalt by marriage, he replies politely. He realizes that you have to put up with a good deal from in-laws.

"Tybalt, you rat-catcher!" † Mercutio says colorfully, whipping out his sword.

"I am for you!" cries Tybalt, trying to mix him up, really being against him.

As they fight, Romeo steps between them, his courage matched only by his stupidity. Tybalt thrusts under Romeo's arm and stabs Mercutio and flies. We are not told what happened to the flies, but Mercutio is in a bad way.

* Perhaps he does, deep down inside where it isn't visible.
† The equivalent of the modern dog-catcher, or man-with-the-net. Anyhow, it's good to know that Tybalt is employed.

Tybalt's underarm thrust

"I am hurt," he groans, in one of the greatest understatements in all Shakespeare.

"Courage, man, the hurt cannot be much," says Romeo, who fails to notice that his friend is standing up to his ankles in blood.

Not until Mercutio is dead does Romeo appreciate the seriousness of the situation. Then he vows to get back at Tybalt * for his underhanded underarm thrust. Completely forgetting about Tybalt's being a relative on his wife's side, Romeo unsheathes, feints, parries, and thrusts. "Tybalt falls," we are told, and in a Shakespearean tragedy this usually means he is dead, which turns out to be the case.

Romeo could be executed for this act of passion, but Benvolio pleads with the Prince, who lets Romeo off easy, merely banishing him for life. To a home-town boy, who believes there is no place like Verona, this is the end.†

Things are a mess

That night Juliet is waiting impatiently for Romeo to come climbing up the rope, hand over hand, and ready to hand over herself. She thinks happily of their life together, and dreams up an unusual way to memorialize her husband.

"When he shall die," she muses sentimentally, "take him and cut him out in little stars." ‡ Apparently she can see herself with a cookie cutter, and bits of Romeo all over the place. She has quite an imagination.

Just then the Nurse arrives with the news that Romeo has

---

* Who has returned to the scene, probably to retrieve his sword, which he left sticking in Mercutio.

† There are, however, three and a half acts still to come.

‡ See, above, what Romeo wanted to do with Juliet's eyes. They both have star fixations.

killed her kinsman, Tybalt, and been banished. At first Juliet shrieks piteously to learn that Tybalt has been slain, and by her husband of all people. She ransacks her vocabulary for suitable epithets to describe Romeo.

"O serpent heart, hid with a flowering face!" she screams, remembering the time he wriggled up the trellis with a long-stemmed rose in each nostril.

But her mood changes. A shudder goes through her frame. She blanches, clutches her breast, and staggers upstage left.

"Some word there was, worser than Tybalt's death," she says to the Nurse, lapsing into the grammar of her age.* Before the Nurse can tell her what it was, she remembers. It was "banished." The tears gush forth more violently than ever, but now in Romeo's direction. After all, she has several cousins but only one husband. Subsiding, Juliet tells the Nurse to give Romeo a ring. Since there are no telephones,

* *Fourteen.*

The Nurse off to Romeo

the poor old soul has to shuffle the weary miles to Friar Laurence's cell, where Romeo is hiding.

Romeo is blue about his banishment,* but cheers up when the Nurse arrives with word that Juliet still loves him, though he must promise never to do anything like that to Tybalt again. He is further cheered when the Friar says that if he will lie low in Mantua for a while, the news of his marriage can be broken gently to old Capulet, who will welcome his son-in-law back with open arms.† Friar Laurence is president of the Optimist Club of Verona.

Romeo returns for one almost idyllic night with Juliet before he hies himself to Mantua. It might have been perfect, indeed, but for a small disagreement. They hear a bird singing, and Juliet says it's a nightingale in a pomegranate tree, while Romeo insists it's a lark in the poison ivy. They argue about this until dawn, and Romeo might have been caught with his ladder down had not the Nurse come in.

"The day is broke," she announces, slaughtering the King's Italian. Romeo takes one last kiss (for the road) and is on his way to Mantua.

Just as things seem to be taking a turn for the better, Juliet gets some bad news. Her mother brings word that she is to marry the County Paris next Thursday.

Juliet is aghast, and feels very little better when she learns that County Paris is only one man. She vows she will not marry him, come Hell or high water, both of which at the moment seem unlikely. What does come is her father, old

---

* *And not helped any by the good Friar's remark, "Thou art wedded to calamity," a tactless thing to say to a bridegroom, whatever he may think of the bride.*

† *Firearms, perhaps.*

Capulet, and when he hears that Juliet won't have Paris, he is furious.

"You baggage!" he cries, swearing he will put handles on her and carry her to church himself, if necessary. Then he gets even uglier. "I will drag thee on a hurdle thither." *

"Fie, fie!" interjects Lady Capulet, whose language is refined and monosyllabic.

"You green-sickness carrion! You tallow-face!" † Capulet shouts, reaching a crescendo of paternal enthusiasm, and more than a little proud of his vocabulary. "Fettle your fine joints 'gainst Thursday next," he says, thinking some deep-knee bends might limber her up. Finally he storms out in a high dudgeon, pulled by two white horses, maintaining that Juliet must marry Paris or else. The alternative is too terrible to relate.

"Do as thou wilt," says Lady Capulet, washing her hands of the affair, and toweling briskly.

But does Juliet wilt? No. She has a lot of spunk, that girl. Things look black, but she will go to Friar Laurence. *He* will know what to do.

A desperate plan

It is now Tuesday, and time is short. If something isn't done by Thursday, Juliet will have two husbands and will be twice as nervous as the usual bride.

But the good Friar has a plan. It is long and intricate and he has obviously been working on it for days, when he should have been praying or gathering weeds.

"Take thou this vial," he tells Juliet. When she goes to bed

* *He doesn't specify high hurdle or low, but either would do.*
† *Juliet still hasn't removed that cold cream.*

Friar Laurence's home brew

Wednesday night, if she will swallow "the distilling liquor," *
it will make her stop breathing, turn cold, and look as good as
dead. "The roses in thy lips and cheeks shall fade to paly
ashes," he says, "and thy eyes' windows fall." He can see it
vividly, even the little shutters in front of her eyes, and is in
an ecstasy of ghoulish delight.

On Thursday morning, the Friar continues, Paris will come
to her bedroom to rouse her and, thinking her deceased,
change his mind about marriage. She will then be borne on a
bier to the Capulet vault and left to become one of the family
skeletons. After forty-two hours (so it says on the label), the
effect of the medicine will wear off and Juliet will wake up
without even a hangover. Meanwhile the Friar will have

* *The Friar does a little medicinal moonshining in back of the cloister.*

posted an epistle to Romeo, explaining the whole complicated business, and Romeo will be right there in the vault * when Juliet awakens, and can carry her off to Mantua.

It's a gruesome scheme, but Juliet is not to be outdone when it comes to thinking up macabre ideas.

"O, bid me leap from off the battlements, chain me with roaring bears, or shut me nightly in a charnel-house," she beseeches the Friar. But he thinks his plan is preferable, having more confidence in poisons.

Juliet trudges homeward, clutching the vial in her hot little hand. Because of her youth, she is unaware that the traditional way to get rid of an unwelcome suitor is to give *him* the poison.

The denouement (how it comes out)

At first everything goes as planned. Juliet shakes well before using, takes a deep draught, and falls on the bed senseless, without even time to slip out of her street clothes. In the morning the Nurse tries to wake her and discovers she is sleeping the Long Sleep.† Lamentation ensues.

"O day! O day!" cries the Nurse.

"O child! O child!" cries Capulet.

"O love! O life" cries Paris, with a little more variety.

The only good thing about the whole affair, as the Father of the Bride ‡ observes, is the fact that the flowers ordered for the wedding will do very nicely for the funeral.

So Juliet, in her burying clothes, is stowed away in the family vault with Tybalt and sundry other decomposed kin-

---

* *Watch in hand, counting off the seconds.*
† *But athwart rather than lengthwise.*
‡ *Henceforth referred to as the Father of the Corpse.*

folk. Pale though she is, she's the best-looking thing in the place.

But now matters go awry. The friar whom Friar Laurence sent "with speed to Mantua" either was arrested for speeding or took a wrong turn. Anyhow, word fails to reach Romeo about Juliet's true condition. He hears that she is dead, and forthwith rushes out and buys some poison of his own. His idea is to imbibe it in the Capulet burial vault, so that at least he can have the pleasure of being dead in the same place with Juliet.

However, when he gets to the tomb and pries his way in with "an iron crow" (either a misprint for "crowbar" or a mighty tough bird), he finds Paris already there. Paris came not to die but to bring flowers, but Romeo changes all that with a few thrusts of his sword. Some of Shakespeare's best dialogue ensues.

ROMEO. Have at thee, boy. [*They fight.*]

PARIS. O, I am slain! [*Falls.*]

Thereupon he dies (also in square brackets), and Romeo turns back to the business at hand. "Here will I remain," he remarks gloomily to the prettiest corpse, "with worms that are thy chamber-maids." The picture conjured up, of worms bustling about with little white caps on their heads, dusting the ledges, is one of Shakespeare's most masterful.

Then, sealing Juliet's lips with a kiss, to keep them water-tight, he quaffs the poison and is dead even before he can make a long speech.*

Just after the nick of time, Friar Laurence arrives with a lantern, another of those iron crows, and a spade. At the same

* *This is the only valid internal evidence that Shakespeare might not have written this play.*

time (exactly forty-two hours, to the second) Juliet awakens refreshed. Seeing the bodies of Paris and Romeo, and figuring everything out at a glance, she snatches up Romeo's dagger.

"O happy dagger!" she says as she thrusts the lucky blade into her bosom. "This is thy sheath; there rust, and let me die." As soon as she can arrange her robe tastefully and fold her hands in the approved manner, she expires. The Friar might have saved her had he not been momentarily distracted by the arrival of the Watch, a large crowd of people who like to stare intently at anything gruesome.

Shortly the tomb is full of sightseers and well-wishers. In a moment of generosity, Montague promises to have a solid-gold statue of Juliet erected in the town square, thereby reminding American tourists of what put Verona on the map.

It's too bad about Romeo and Juliet, but anyhow Montague

The tomb is full

and Capulet bury the hatchet.* They exeunt arm in arm, hand in glove, and tongue in cheek.†

* *And not, as might have been anticipated earlier, in each other.*
† *Legend has it that they went into business together, selling postcards and souvenirs.*

1. Which would you rather be:

   a. A Montague?
   b. A Capulet?
   c. A. Rose by any other name?

2. Lady Capulet refers to Paris as "This precious book of love, this unbound volume." What was he really like, when you read between the lines?
3. Didn't you think Escalus was a Greek?
4. Discuss one of the following:

   a. Star-crossed lovers.
   b. Moon-struck lovers.
   c. Cross-eyed mooners.

5. Which would be preferable, being stabbed to death by Tybalt or talked to death by the Nurse?
6. Some scholars maintain that Juliet had no balcony. Did she have a bay window?
7. As Juliet ran her fingers through Romeo's hair, she murmured, "Parting is such sweet sorrow." Would a comb and brush have helped?
8. Can you tell the difference between a lark and a nightingale in the dark? In a meat pie?
9. After viewing the corpses of Romeo and Juliet, express your candid opinion of the critic who said that "at the close of the play both hero and heroine are stronger and finer than at the beginning."

The Merchant
of Venice

Introduction

The direct source of The Merchant of Venice *is a play which has not survived. It was sick to start with, and passed away around 1570. The casket story came from the medieval* Gesta Romanorum, *or* Jests of the Romans, *and was probably funnier in the original. The idea of a woman dressing up like a man * and practicing law came from Italy and may have returned there. The pound of flesh came from a butcher shop and has been associated with Bologna.*

The earliest recorded performance of The Merchant of Venice *was before King James I on February 10, 1605. He ordered a second performance two days later, hoping against hope that he would get the point this time.*

As many have observed, the plot of The Merchant of Venice *is well knit, which proves that it is a work of Shakespeare's maturity. In his early years, Shakespeare would not have been caught dead knitting a plot. By the time he was forty, however, he didn't care what people thought, and the good citizens of London could hear his needles clicking far into the night.*

* *The very ideal*

The trial scene is the most exciting part, and suggests that Shakespeare may well have learned about the court firsthand (see General Introduction for poaching incident). He may even have spent some time in prison for forging the name of Francis Bacon or contributing to the delinquency of playgoers by writing works like Titus Andronicus.

As for the characterization in The Merchant of Venice, an eminent scholar asserts that "the people are human." This is a good thing, because people of any other kind would make it something of a problem for actors. Portia, a truly charming lady, was lifted from a play by Marlowe, and the original rope and pulley may be seen in the Folger Shakespeare Library in Washington, D.C.

With regard to literary type, The Merchant of Venice is a tragicomedy, a term which will be readily understood by persons familiar with comitragedy. That it contains a moral is clear, or at least clearer than what the moral is.

As one critic has said with great discernment, "The Merchant of Venice is not one of Shakespeare's greatest plays, nor is it one of his worst." What could be truer? What safer?

The Merchant of Venice

Bassanio needs cash

Antonio, the merchant of Venice in *The Merchant of Venice*, is waiting for his ships to come in. He has invested almost all his money in Venetian bottoms,* which are tossing around on the ocean somewhere.

At this inopportune time, his friend Bassanio comes to him for a loan, and Antonio is touched. What Bassanio, who is wooing the fair Portia, needs is enough ducats to press his suit and maybe buy a new pair of pants. He has been kneeling at her feet, and his knickers have taken a beating.

"The four winds blow in from every coast renownèd suitors," explains Bassanio, painting a vivid picture of the air full of eligible young men. And all of them, it seems, are more fashionably attired than he. Without at least a new cravat, he hasn't a chance.

But he is hopeful. "Sometimes from her eyes I did receive fair speechless messages," he tells Antonio. By this he means to say, albeit wordily, that she occasionally winks at him, though there is always the possibility that it's only a nervous twitch. Anyhow, he needs a couple of lire if he is to treat her to a pizza now and then.

"Thou know'st that all my fortunes are at sea," Antonio

* See the expression "bottom dollar."

replies sadly, trying to explain that even if he does get his money back it will take weeks for it to dry out before it will be negotiable. However, he says his credit is good and he will try to borrow some money to help Bassanio with Portia. (Here an obscure reference is made to "Belmont, Portia's seat." They named *everything* in those days.)

The pound of flesh

Bassanio and Antonio visit a moneylender named Shylock,* a man whose only interest is interest. They want three thousand ducats for three months, and are willing to put up Antonio as collateral.

"How like a fawning publican † he looks," says Shylock, referring to Antonio, in a loud voice which everyone but Antonio and Bassanio can hear. This is an Aside, an Elizabethan device which made it possible to talk behind people's backs in front of them.‡ The reason Shylock says nasty things about Antonio is that the latter is always lending people money without charging them interest, which is Unfair to Moneylenders. To a man like Shylock, who pays dues to the union, this isn't cricket.

Finally Shylock says he'll lend the money, but on condition that if it isn't repaid at the stipulated time, Antonio will have to give him a pound of flesh cut off from whatever part of his body Shylock selects. As he says this, Shylock looks Antonio over from head to foot, and asks him to turn around slowly please.

Antonio agrees to Shylock's terms, confident that his ships

---

* *In some texts, Shyalock, which suggests semibaldness.*

† *Republicans please read: "How like a fawning mocrat he looks."*

‡ *An Aside may also be defined as a whisper that can be heard in the last row in the balcony.*

will be back with plenty of money within a month. Bassanio, however, is uneasy, thinking his friend may be penny wise and pound foolish. They go to a notary to have it all made legal, and "Reserved" is stamped on the more solid portions of Antonio's anatomy.

The three caskets

Portia is an extremely eligible young woman, having beauty, brains, wit, inventiveness, and so much money that the afore-mentioned qualities are superfluous. Her father has left her not only a handsome dowry but an ingenious way of weeding out her suitors. There are three caskets (not counting Father's), one of gold, one of silver, and one of lead. In order to win Portia, a suitor has to guess which one contains her picture, and no prompting from the audience.*

* *"Which casket?" came to be known as the 64,000-Ducat Question. Many went around humming the hit tune, "A tisket, a tasket. What's in the golden casket?"*

One day, with a flourish of cornets (cornets seem to be flourishing at this time, or at least doing better than trombones), the Prince of Morocco comes in for a try at the caskets. He is dark of hue, and gets some black looks.

"Mislike me not for my complexion," he begs, putting the best light on it, "the shadowed livery of the burnished sun." (Sun spots, apparently, or liver spots.)

"Now make your choice, Prince," she tells him, pointing to the three caskets. "The one of them contains my picture. If you choose that, then I am yours withal." He seems to know withal what, and needs no further encouragement.

Each casket bears an inscription. On the gold one it's "Who chooseth me shall gain what many men desire." This sounds

The casket game

good to the Prince, who chooses it forthwith. Alas, the casket may be golden, but the inscription is irony. Inside, the Prince finds not Portia's portrait but a scroll and crossbones. On the scroll is written "All that glisters is not gold." The Prince is chagrined. All these years he has been saying "glistens." He heads back to Morocco with a heavy heart, almost more than his horse can bear.

The heavy-hearted prince

The second suitor is the Prince of Aragon, an arrogant fellow who picks the silver casket because of its inscription, "Who chooseth me shall get as much as he deserves." He gets his desserts, it's true, but quickly loses his appetite.

"What's here? The portrait of a blinking idiot!" he cries with dismay. It's obviously not Portia, unless perchance her passport photo. But, although he has flubbed his chance, he has a sense of humor and quickly dashes off a little poem:

"With one fool's head I came to woo,
But now I go away with two."

He doesn't get Portia, but he gets as good a laugh as anybody in the play.

The third suitor is Bassanio, the only one Portia really loves. "One half of me is yours, the other half yours," she tells him cryptically, hoping he can add. She wishes she could give him a subtle hint, such as pointing to the right casket.

"Let me choose," says Bassanio impatiently, "for as I am, I live upon the rack." He is stretching things a little.

While Bassanio deliberates, and Portia chews her fingernails, an orchestra furnishes background music. Bassanio hums along with it and breaks into the chorus of a song popular in Venetian bakeries, "Tell me where is fancy bread?" Portia joins him in the beautiful refrain, "Ding, dong, bell." *

Passing over the gold and silver caskets, Bassanio chooses the leaden one, rather liking its cheery inscription: "Who chooseth me must give and hazard all he hath." He has nothing to lose, being flat broke.

Inside the casket Bassanio finds a picture which is unmistakably that of Portia. He is ecstatic, recognizing those "sever'd lips, parted with sugar breath." Nevertheless he is a little startled at what he finds in her hair.

"Here, in her hairs," he says, "the painter plays the spider, and hath woven a golden mesh to entrap the hearts of men faster than gnats in cobwebs."

While Bassanio is removing the entangled painter, it is

* "Hark, isn't that Our Song?" they will say in later years whenever they hear it played at one of the sidewalk cafés on the Piazza San Marco.

116

Portia's turn to make a passionate speech. We overcome without difficulty the impulse to quote it in full.

"Madam," Bassanio replies, "you have bereft me of all words. Only my blood speaks to you in my veins." Apparently thereafter he must rely on short and long pulse beats for communication.

Portia takes a ring from her finger and puts it on Bassanio's as a symbol of their troth.

"When this ring parts from this finger," Bassanio swears, "then parts life from hence." What he means is that the ring is such a tight fit, the only way to remove it will be by amputation.

All is happiness, but just then a cloud darkens Bassanio's brow. It's not a change in the weather; he has received a letter from Antonio that is, frankly, disturbing.

"Here are a few of the unpleasant'st words that ever blotted paper!" Bassanio exclaims, after deciphering the messy epistle. It seems that Antonio's ships have gone down and his fortunes are on the rocks. Shylock has been seen smacking his lips and looking for his whetstone.

Bassanio hastens to his friend's side, expecting to see a gaping hole therein. He might have said, were Shakespeare not saving the line for *Julius Caesar*, "This was the most unkindest cut of all."

Shylock has his troubles

Lest Shylock be thought a hard man without cause, it should be pointed out that he has been having a hell of a time. His servant, Launcelot Gobbo, who doubles as a clown, is leaving Shylock to take a job with Bassanio, and with the servant problem what it is—well, really!

Still worse, Shylock's daughter, Jessica, disguised as a page and making a folio of herself, runs off with Lorenzo, a friend of Bassanio's. Before she takes her leave, she takes as much of her father's jewelry and cash as she can stagger away with.*

"I will make fast the doors, and gild myself with some more ducats, and be with you straight," Jessica calls down from the window to her waiting swain.

Lorenzo tells her not to hurry, but to go right on gilding herself. As for her coming to him straight, he doesn't mind if she bends a little under all that load of valuables. She'll straighten out later.

When Shylock discovers his loss he is distraught. "My daughter! O my ducats! O my daughter!" he screams as he splashes his way up and down the canals of Venice. Jessica

The original "cash and carry" plan.

Exeunt Jessica and ducats

118

and Lorenzo are rumored to have escaped by gondola, and Shylock is the only one who doesn't think this romantic.

Portia's Day in court

Antonio is arrested and haled before the Duke, who is also a judge, to show cause why he shouldn't pay Shylock the pound of flesh.

"I am sorry for thee," says the Duke. "Thou art come to answer a stony adversary, an inhuman wretch, uncapable of pity, void and empty from any dram of mercy." The Duke doesn't like Shylock, but he is careful not to let on, because a judge must be impartial.

Shylock is brought in. A spontaneous hiss arises from the packed courtroom. Antonio has a bad case of goose pimples. It is a Tense Moment.

Extra ducats are offered Shylock in lieu of the pound of flesh. But he will accept no substitutes. "It is my humor," he says, meaning that he gets a laugh out of cutting up. "A certain loathing I bear Antonio," he adds, to show that they aren't exactly buddies. Then he goes back to whetting his knife on the edge of the witness stand.

At this point a learned Doctor named Balthazar arrives in court, so learned that he is not only a doctor but a lawyer, and takes over the case. Actually this legal eagle is none other than Portia in disguise. She has on a man's raiment (probably a lawsuit) and by some unexplained means has lowered her voice a couple of octaves, broadened her shoulders, and sprouted a beard. With her is Nerissa, her waiting woman,*

* It may have been during periods of waiting that she picked up the learned language she uses in the last two acts.

dressed like a lawyer's clerk and also looking too masculine for words.*

"The quality of mercy is not strained," Portia declares as she cross-examines Shylock. And then, to confuse him still further, she remarks enigmatically, "It droppeth as the gentle rain from heaven upon the place beneath."

"My deeds upon my head!" Shylock cries, so overcome by the poetic beauty of her speech that he reveals the hiding place of his legal papers, under his hat.

Although she doesn't know a habeas from a corpus,† and is irrelevant, immaterial, and implausible, Portia impresses the judge (who, remember, is only a Duke) with her knowledge of the law.

But, observing that she isn't getting anywhere with Shylock, who is playing mumblety-peg on the bench, she suddenly tells him to go ahead and take his pound of flesh, and from a spot as close as possible to Antonio's heart. Then, turning to Antonio, she instructs him to make ready. "Lay bare your bosom," she says, meaning his chest or perhaps thinking everyone in court who is dressed up like a man is a woman.

Though Antonio seems less than enthusiastic, Shylock is exceedingly happy. He has always had a secret desire to be a surgeon, and now he has arrived at the hour of incision. He calls for a scalpel, forceps, and gauze. Just as he is slipping into his rubber gloves, Portia offers a word of caution.

"Shed thou no blood," she warns him, "nor cut thou less, nor more, but just a pound of flesh. Nay, if the scale do turn

---

* The only words used by Shakespeare are "Dressed like a lawyer's clerk." As far as he was concerned, that did it.

† And thinks a plaintiff is the same thing as a commonquarrel.

but in the estimation of a hair, thou diest and all thy goods are confiscate." Being a woman, she knows how hard it is for a butcher to come within two pounds when weighing a three-pound roast, and looks around triumphantly, awaiting applause.

"Is that the law?" asks Shylock, suddenly wishing he had read all the fine print. Caught without a cauterizing agent, he sees the game is up. He thinks of throwing himself on the mercy of the court, but one look at the judge convinces him that he would land on the floor.

"Give me my principal," he begs, "and let me go." This is the first time he has given any evidence of principal, and it's too late.* By the time Portia gets through with him, proving he has threatened attack with a deadly weapon, he gives up half his wealth to the state. Then he exits on the famous line, "I am not well."

Portia, despite all her cleverness in court, proves that she doesn't know the first thing about law by refusing a fee of 3,000 ducats. "He is well paid that is well satisfied," she remarks, quoting some sage who knows his philosophy better than his economics. All she wants is the ring that Bassanio swore he would never take off his finger. This she gets, after some wheedling and not a little tugging and twisting.

The ring

Portia gets home before Bassanio, resumes her female figure, and slips it into a diaphanous gown. When Bassanio arrives, tired from a long day of worry over Antonio's pound of flesh, she greets him with the demand that he show her the ring

* *Almost the end of Act IV.*

What!—No ring?

she gave him. (This, according to critics, is an example of her gentle, mocking wit. She is Shakespeare's first Complex Character.)

"It is gone," says Bassanio, who cannot tell a lie, or cannot think of one on such short notice.

"By heaven, I will ne'er come in your bed until I see the ring," Portia threatens, falling back on one of woman's oldest devices.

Bassanio goes all to pieces. "Pardon this fault," he blubbers. "I nevermore will break an oath with thee."

Finally Portia has had enough of her little joke, but not until long after the reader. She explains about being disguised as the lawyer, besting Shylock, and getting the ring. Bassanio is surprised and relieved, but a little apprehensive. Henceforth, as he can see, Portia is going to wear the pants, and not merely in court.

But Portia hasn't finished. "It is almost morning, and yet I am sure you are not satisfied of these events at full," she says. She is really wound up, and good for several hours more of unimportant details and repetition. We are luckier than Bassanio, however, because the play ends here.

Odds and ends

If anyone is interested, it might be added that Antonio's ships didn't sink after all, or not permanently. Three of them limped into port with an extra-heavy cargo of gold bullion.* The report of their loss was an error on the part of an inexperienced lighthouse keeper who had seen them drop over the horizon. But it was a lucky break for Shakespeare, who would otherwise have been left without a plot.

As for Shylock, nothing further is said of him, and we can only surmise. Did he go back to usury? † Did he try some quicker way to make money, such as counterfeiting? Did he ever perform an appendectomy? All we know is that he eventually became a household word, known by millions of people who have never read *The Merchant of Venice*.

Questions on The Merchant of Venice

1. Was it Antonio who coined the expression, "When the ships are down"?
2. Haven't you always thought that Shylock was the merchant of Venice? Now be honest.
3. Think of several names that are funnier than Launcelot Gobbo. (There is always Greta Gobbo.)

In the form of bullion cubes.
†*For better or for worsery.*

4. Which do you think is the more important motivating force in the play, (a) Shylock or (b) wedlock?
5. Point to the Rialto Bridge on a map. Unless it is a map of Venice, this won't be easy.
6. "She hath stones upon her," says Shylock of Jessica. Visualize this scene. You might get some help from reading Ruskin's three-volume treatise, *The Stones of Venice*.
7. If the quality of mercy is not strained, how is it kept from being lumpy?
8. Did you ever hear of a woman lawyer who wasn't, at one time or another, called a Portia? What are men lawyers called, especially by their convicted clients?

OTHELLO

Introduction

Scholars have long believed that Shakespeare derived the plot of Othello *from an Italian novel. However we are now able to assert that he took it from the Irish tale of O'Thello and Tess Demona, a touching story in which a woman marries beneath her station.**

Othello *is another work of Shakespeare's maturity. For evidence, scholars point to the number of feminine endings (Desdemona and Emilia both killed), and the matchless way in which Shakespeare fires the emotions, usually by rubbing two pieces of dry wit together. There is also the admirable precision which results when, as a careful count reveals, the exits exactly equal the entrances, except in the case of dead bodies.†*

That Othello *is a late work is further indicated by the fact that, Shakespeare having run out of gravediggers, gatekeepers, and ghosts, there is no comic relief. In fact only the final curtain brings any relief whatsoever.*

* *Her lover belonged to the Irish underground.*
† *A case of bodies is a gruesome thing, God wot.*

One matter concerning the text should be mentioned. Because of an Act of Parliament, all the curses were cut out of the first quarto, leaving it a patchwork of four-letter holes. These made the Puritans happy and challenged everyone else's imagination.

In literary type, Othello is a domestic tragedy; that is, a realistic account of married life in Venice during the sixteenth century. It shows how a woman may start out being smothered

with kisses and end up just being smothered. As one critic has remarked, "Shakespeare wove the threads of the plot together," which evokes a picture of the poet busy at his loom, trying to remember which is the warp and which is the woof.

By far the most fascinating character is Iago, the villain of the piece. He is so complex that he must be studied at various levels, and the reader is advised to bring a ladder. Iago manipulates Othello in ways that are obvious to us but not seen by Othello until the fifth act, when his eyes are opened.*

* They close again shortly after he stabs himself.

Othello is a favorite vehicle of the stage, almost as popular as the dolly and the wheelbarrow. It may be of no interest whatever to learn that the part of Desdemona was the first ever played on the English public stage by a woman. Subsequently it was played by many famous actresses, including Mrs. Brace-girdle, a charming lady who retired from the stage after failing in heroic attempts to keep her figure.

𝕴𝖆𝖌𝖔 𝖘𝖙𝖆𝖗𝖙𝖘 𝖒𝖆𝖐𝖎𝖓𝖌 𝖙𝖗𝖔𝖚𝖇𝖑𝖊

The play is set in Venice, probably so that the costumes and stage properties of *The Merchant of Venice* can be used over again. Roderigo, referred to as "a gulled gentleman" because the birds have made a mess of him, is talking in the street with his friend Iago. Iago, according to the list of characters, is a villain. This is his specialty, and he works hard at it, but he is also a Venetian soldier with the rank of ancient.* He is on the staff of a general named Othello and has been bucking for a lieutenancy, but Othello has given the spot to another officer, Cassio.

"Who is this Cassio?" Iago sneers. Cassio, he makes clear, is a desk soldier, with leather patches on his elbows, while he himself has overseas stripes from his wrist to his shoulder. As for Othello, "I follow him to serve my turn upon him," says Iago slyly. "Not I for love and duty, but seeming so, for my peculiar end." Why he would call attention to this abnormality is not explained.

Iago then tells Roderigo a juicy bit of news: Othello, a Moor with a deep sunburn and African relatives, has secretly married the beautiful Desdemona. Even her own father, Brabantio, hasn't an inkling, though if his daughter and

* *A title given to officers who are advanced in age but not in rank.*

Cassio is a desk soldier

Othello beget offspring he may have one for a grandchild. Roderigo, who had hoped to win the fair Desdemona himself, is now a Disappointed Suitor.

"Call up her father," Iago tells his friend, thinking there must be a phone booth somewhere on the Grand Canal. And then, with reference to Othello, "Make after him, poison his delight, plague him with flies." Iago is never at a loss for suggestions.

Although it is very late, they rout Brabantio from his bed and soon have him running around looking for Desdemona in his nightgown.*

Told that his daughter has eloped, Brabantio cries out, "Get weapons, ho! And raise some special officers of the night." He can hardly wait to see his new son-in-law.

* *An unlikely place for her.*

A few hours later, the Duke of Venice sits on the case of Brabantio vs. Othello. The court just happens to be in night session, trying to clear up a crowded calendar.

"With some dram he wrought upon her," Brabantio charges, insisting that Othello must have slipped a love potion * into his daughter's *cafe espresso* while she was peering into his large brown eyes. Otherwise she would never have married a man with a "sooty bosom."

Ignoring the reference to his personal cleanliness, Othello denies the accusation. "Rude am I in my speech," he apologizes, thereupon launching upon one of the most eloquent courtroom defenses in English literature. All he did, apparently, was to tell Desdemona stories about his travels and about the strange people he met, such as "men whose heads do grow beneath their shoulders" and therefore have no use for a collar and tie. For her part, Desdemona testifies that she married Othello because she loved to hear him talk about himself, thereby establishing herself as the Perfect Wife.

The Duke acquits Othello and urges Brabantio to go home and forget about the whole business, or to put his shoes on if he insists on tramping around Venice all night. "He robs himself that spends a bootless grief," he remarks wisely.

Roderigo is as dejected as Brabantio. "I will incontinently drown myself," he says glumly to Iago, apparently planning to go down somewhere between Europe and Africa.

"A pox of drowning thyself!" says Iago. He advises Rod to drown cats and blind puppies if he's bent on drowning things. It will afford just as much satisfaction without getting him so wet.

---

* *Possibly there was a little left over from* A Midsummer Night's Dream.

Having sent Roderigo packing, Iago mumbles to himself about how he will "abuse Othello's ear," possibly by filling it brimful of lies about Cassio's being familiar with Desdemona. He hopes that his stories of Cassio's familiarity will breed Othello's contempt.

It is obvious * that Iago is up to no good.

Cassio is cashiered

The scene shifts to Cyprus, where Othello has become a hero by defeating the Turkish navy, materially assisted by a storm which sinks all the Turkish ships and makes it unnecessary to fire a shot. All this is the more amazing since Othello is a general and not an admiral.

Iago, Desdemona, Cassio, and the others join the victorious Othello in Cyprus.† Once, when Cassio is talking to Desdemona, he gallantly kisses her hand, and Iago thinks she is beginning to knuckle under.

"Well kiss'd," he hisses softly, relishing each sibilant syllable. "With as little a web as this will I ensnare as great a fly as Cassio." Cassio buzzes off. Iago also exits, making like a spider.

That night, when Cassio is in charge of the guard, Iago persuades him to drink a stoup ‡ of wine. Toasting the marriage of Othello and Desdemona, Iago declares, "Well, happiness to their sheets." This is doubtless a slip of the tongue,

* *To all but the slow student.*
† *Otherwise, with Othello in Cyprus and everybody else in Venice, the play would be difficult for even Shakespeare to manage.*
‡ *A large glass, enough to make a man stoupid.*

caused by too much Chianti, because Iago must have meant to refer to the happiness of the bride and groom.

As for Cassio, he becomes inebriated and very nearly drunk, although he stoutly denies it. "This is my right hand, and thish is my left," he says, shrewdly realizing that he has a fifty-fifty chance. "And I can stand well enough," he boasts, sprawling on the floor.*

According to plan, Roderigo then engages Cassio in a duel, but an innocent bystander is the one to feel the steel.

"Help, ho! Diablo, ho," cries Iago, summoning a friend.

But it is Othello who appears on the scene. Noticing that Cassio is as drunk as a lord when he is only a lieutenant, he dismisses him.

"Cassio, I love thee," he says sorrowfully, "but never more be officer of mine." Othello uses the word "love" loosely, this quite plainly being a dishonorable discharge.

Left alone with Iago, Cassio feels terrible. Seldom has he had such a hangover. Besides, he may have lost not only his job but his veteran's benefits.

"Reputation, reputation, reputation! Oh, I have lost my reputation," Cassio moans. He refers to his reputation for holding liquor, to an Army man a serious blow indeed.

Iago does some insinuating

Iago, now scheming around the clock,† persuades Cassio to ask Desdemona to use her influence to get him reinstated.

Desdemona, who is very kindhearted and slow-witted,

---

* At this point Shakespeare is mixing low comedy with high tragedy, and the result is what might be expected.

† Three eight-hour shifts.

swears she will pester Othello until he gives in. "My lord shall never rest," she declares. "I'll intermingle everything he does with Cassio's suit."

And so she does. Othello finds Cassio's suit in his closet, between two of his uniforms, and the effect is not what Desdemona intended.

"Nay," she says when he airs his suspicions. "When I have a suit wherein I mean to touch your love indeed, it shall be full of poise and difficult weight." Does she mean that Cassio will be in it?

Othello is worried, and unburdens himself about the whole disagreeable business to Iago, who is not the best confidant under the circumstances. But Othello doesn't know the circumstances.

Isn't it a little strange, Iago asks, that Desdemona would go to all this trouble for Cassio if he is only a passing acquaintance? People are beginning to talk.*

Othello is not prone to jealousy, but Iago's insinuations at last get under his skin, causing an odd form of dermatitis. He thinks he has horns growing out of his forehead, and calls Desdemona in to help remove them. Desdemona sees no horns, but, to humor him, binds her husband's head in a napkin which she has been using as a handkerchief.

This napkin suddenly becomes an important character in the play, causing no end of trouble. It drops from Othello's head and falls into Iago's hands. (Apparently he was lying on the floor, waiting.) It is a very special napkin, "spotted with strawberries," † which Othello gave to Desdemona when they were courting and which she swore never to give up, even to

* And no one more than Iago.

† Jam, very likely.

134

Othello thinks he has horns

send to the laundry. But Iago passes it through his wife, Emilia, to Cassio, and he to his mistress, whom one day Othello sees wiping her brow with it, strawberry spots and all. Othello thinks it downright unsanitary.

"That's *our* napkin," he sobs. And he remembers what an unusual napkin it is. "The worms were hallowed that did breed the silk," he says awesomely, picturing the little group of pious silkworms at work. It is almost more than he can bear.

Nor is this all. Iago, just warming up, tells Othello a whopper about sleeping with Cassio one night, one or the other of them having gotten into the wrong bed, and how Cassio moaned in his sleep about his love for Desdemona.

"I heard him say, 'Sweet Desdemona, let us be wary, let us hide our loves.' And then, sir, would he gripe and wring my hand, cry, 'O sweet creature!' and then kiss me hard, as if he pluck'd up kisses by the roots." Shakespeare doesn't say what Cassio had to gripe about, at least until he woke up and discovered he was in bed with Iago.

"O monstrous! monstrous!" Othello cries. "I'll tear her all to pieces! O, blood, blood, blood!" He is obviously upset.

Iago makes Othello even surer of Desdemona's unfaithfulness by hiding him out of earshot while Cassio is talking about Bianca, a girl friend of his who, as Iago says, is "a housewife that by selling her desires buys herself bread and clothes." She probably has some other job to supply meat and vegetables.

Anyhow, Bianca is a loose woman, and when Cassio talks of her he makes gestures as if to hold her together. Othello thinks he is talking about Desdemona, and is understandably annoyed. He is convinced that the relationship between Cassio

Cassio describing Bianca

and Desdemona is more than Platonic, possibly even Aristotelian. In his rage, he calls Desdemona a "strumpet" and is about to call her a French whorn and a base viol when he "falls into a trance," from which Iago extricates him with some difficulty.

Back on his feet, Othello senses that something is wrong. "My heart is turned to stone," he says anxiously, having tried unsuccessfully to feel his pulse. Then, remembering Desdemona, "I will chop her into messes!" he screams.

But Iago, who blanches at the sight of blood, has a better idea. "Strangle her in bed," he suggests hopefully.

"Excellent good," exclaims Othello, grabbing a bedpost and beginning to get himself in trim. Now it's only a matter of time, and they check their watches. Iago agrees to finish off Cassio while Othello is disposing of Desdemona, and they go their separate ways, Othello flexing his fingers suggestively.

Almost everybody gets killed

As soon as night falls, Iago stations Roderigo in a dark doorway where he can ambush Cassio when he passes. "Fear nothing," Iago reassures his friend. "I'll be at thy elbow." He gives him ample elbowroom, however, for the stage direction says that the brave fellow "Retires."

As Cassio comes by, Roderigo whispers, "I know his gait, 'tis he." Apparently his gait squeaks a little. At this point, we are told, Roderigo "Makes a pass at Cassio." No wonder Cassio, who doesn't care for this sort of thing, draws his sword and defends himself.

In the melee that follows, Cassio wounds Roderigo, and Iago, seeing that things aren't going as planned, darts out and wounds Cassio in the leg and exits.

"I am maim'd!" cries Cassio, announcing his state of health

in the accustomed manner of participants in a Shakespearean duel. A few minutes later, reappraising his condition, he revises this to "I am spoil'd." *

Shortly afterward, a crowd having gathered, Iago returns "in his shirt," as if roused from sleep by all the hullabaloo and too hurried to put on anything more. Trying to be helpful, he stabs his friend Roderigo to death, pretending not to recognize him in the dark, though he was close enough to see the bags under his eyes. When they drag Roderigo's body under the light, Iago feigns surprise, but cannot hide his amusement.

"He, he," he giggles, " 'tis he."

* See also, in Romeo and Juliet, Mercutio's "I am hurt" (III,ii,93), and in Hamlet, Gertrude's "I am poison'd" (V,ii,321), the King's "I am but hurt" (V,ii,335), Laertes' "I am kill'd" (V,ii,318), and Hamlet's "I am dead" (V,ii,224).

Desdemona prepares for bed

Meanwhile Desdemona prepares for bed, singing her famous "Willow" song, the one that goes "Willow, willow, willow, willow, willow, willow" and so on (and on), until she falls asleep, exhausted. She even sings the part that is plainly marked "Refrain."

When all is quiet, Othello creeps in. "She must die," he mutters, "yet I'll not shed her blood, nor scar that whiter skin of hers than snow, and smooth as monumental alablaster." He means to say "alabaster," blut is understandably distraught.*

Othello gives Desdemona a kiss. Then, overcome by her "balmy breath," he gives her another and another. He is beginning to grow a little balmy himself.

Though a sound sleeper, Desdemona is eventually awakened by all this osculation. As she looks up into her husband's face, she thinks something is wrong and is right. "I fear you when your eyes roll so," she says. "Alas, why gnaw you so your nether lip? Some bloody passion shakes your very frame." She is eloquent, all right, but should have saved her breath for a dash down the hall.

"I hope you will not kill me," she adds wistfully.

"Hum," remarks Othello, not wishing to commit himself.†

"Kill me tomorrow; let me live tonight!" Desdemona begs. She was always one to procrastinate.

But Othello is not to be stayed. "It is too late," he says regretfully, meaning that it is almost tomorrow already. His only concession, at this point, is that he smothers her instead of strangling her.

Just as he finishes the job, Iago's wife, Emilia, who is Desdemona's maid, comes in to see what all the shouting is

---

* We cannot agree with scholars who interpret this as the old Moorish oath, "Allah, blast her!"

† Or could he be ordering Desdemona to start singing again?

about. "O, who hath done this deed?" she asks, meanwhile looking straight at Othello, who is standing over Desdemona, pressing a pillow on her face.

"Nobody," says Desdemona, who comes alive long enough to make a short speech and bid everyone farewell. Then she dies again, and no one can get another word out of her.

"Help! help! ho! help!" Emilia cries out. Despite Desdemona's posthumous testimony, she has an uneasy feeling that Othello is somehow implicated.

Help comes promptly, in the form of Iago and various members of the Venetian Senate.*

"O! O! O!" cries Othello, falling on the bed and adding to the general disorder.

Gradually the truth comes out concerning Iago's treachery. So much of it comes out of his wife Emilia that Iago runs her through with his sword, thus silencing her except for a couple of brief statements for the record and one chorus of the "Willow" song.

"Blow me about in winds! Roast me in sulphur!" Othello shrieks, thoroughly dissatisfied with himself. Then, although he has apparently been disarmed and disrobed, he cries, "Naked as I am, I will assault thee," and lunges at Iago with a sword kept hanging on the wall for just such an emergency.

"I bleed, sir, but not kill'd," Iago reports dutifully to his superior. By this time Iago is in the custody of the police, who are beginning to think him a troublemaker.

"I am not sorry, neither," says Othello, now devoid of all sense of compassion and grammatical construction.

The police grapple with Othello for his sword but the Moor,

---

* *From the speed with which they enter, one gathers that the Senate was in session in the adjoining room.*

140

who is always prepared, has an extra dagger up his sleeve. Using this as a pointer, he tells the assembled notables, "Here is my journey's end, here is my butt." Then, having misled them with these interesting anatomical references, he plunges the dagger into his heart and falls on the bed beside Desdemona. Luckily it is a double bed, wide enough for two corpses.*

Although dead, Othello defies the conventions of Elizabethan drama and makes no further speeches.

As for Iago, he is led off to be punished as soon as someone can think up a suitably gruesome torture. Everyone leaves in a thoughtful mood.

---

* *"A bloody period!" comments one of the minor characters, possibly referring to the Age of Shakespeare.*

The end of a long, hard day

⚜ Questions on Othello

1. Are you too depressed, after reading this play, to answer questions on it?
2. Iago says he is not one to wear his heart upon his sleeve. Was this because it was against Army regulations?
3: "Enter, below, Brabantio, in his nightgown, and servants with torches," reads one stage direction. Wasn't this a risky way for Brabantio to keep warm?
4. Another interesting stage direction reads: "They draw on both sides." Was there a shortage of paper in Venice?
5. Make a detailed comparison of the following speeches by Othello:

   a. "The handkerchief!" (III,iv,92)
   b. "The handkerchief!" (III,iv,93)
   c. "The handkerchief!" (III,iv,96)

6. Several times we are told, "Trumpets within." Could it have been all this blowing of horns, rather than Iago's hinting, that finally caused Othello to crack up?
7. "Her hand on her bosom, her head on her knee,
   Sing willow, willow, willow."
   Try singing *any* song in this position.
8. Was it tactful of Desdemona to say, in Othello's presence, that she was slain by "nobody"?
9. Considering all Iago did, including spreading lies, stealing handkerchiefs, getting people drunk, murdering, and inciting murder, don't you think there must be some easier way to become a lieutenant?

APPENDICES

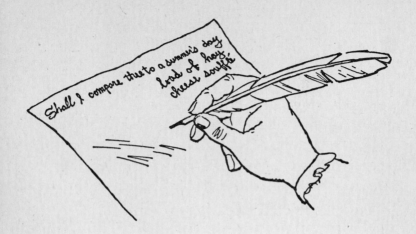

⫸ The Sonnets

Sonnets are of two types: (1) Shakespearean and (2) Petrarchan. Another way of classifying them is (1) Good and (2) Bad. Sonnets may be easily recognized,* because they contain fourteen lines. Occasionally a poet has written a sonnet that was a little shorter, because he could think of nothing more to say, or a little longer, because he was being paid by the line.

The Shakespearean sonnet ends with a Couplet,† which is not to be confused with a Capulet. Anyone who can quote the first two lines and say "and so forth" usually gets credit for knowing the rest. Shakespeare, cognizant of the fact that

---

* *By anyone who can count.*

† *I wish it had been Shakespeare who said, "I have been cohabiting with the Muse, and we are about to have couplets," so that I might quote it here.*

readers tire quickly, customarily put his best line at the beginning.

The opening line of one of Shakespeare's sonnets, the one beautifully entitled "XVIII," is "Shall I compare thee to a summer's day?" * Having posed this interesting question, Shakespeare wisely does not answer it. Then there is the opening of "XXX," the delightful if almost incomprehensible line, "When to the sessions of sweet silent thought," which probably refers to the fact that the nicest thoughts are the syrupy ones. Another memorable line, or line and a half, from "CXVI," is "Let me not to the marriage of true minds admit impediments." Here one has a vivid picture of Shakespeare standing at the door of the church, checking on invitees and keeping out the riffraff.

Shakespeare's sonnets were dedicated to Mr. W.H., at least initially. In those days poems were always dedicated to patrons, and Shakespeare didn't dedicate his sonnets to Mr. W.H. for nothing, though we have no idea how much he got. Mr. W.H., by the way, is referred to as "the onlie begetter," which, if taken in the Biblical sense, implies that he had a monopoly on fatherhood in Elizabethan England and must have been terribly busy.

There are CLIV sonnets, plainly numbered I through CLIV.† Taken all together, they make up what is called a sonnet sequence, popular among Elizabethan poets, such as Sidney and Spenser, who in hard times gave them to their mistresses instead of jewelry. In the Victorian period, when things were quite different, Elizabeth Barrett Browning gave a sonnet sequence to her husband, Robert Browning, but not in lieu of a stickpin.

* *Hot? Sweaty? Fly infested?*
† *Further evidence of Shakespeare's orderly mind.*

One group of Shakespeare's sonnets is addressed to a "dark lady" who is going to Bath, presumably to see whether scrubbing will do anything for her complexion. Another group is addressed to a young man, or "dark laddy." Shakespeare seems to have been fond of both the young man and the young woman, and they in turn seem to have grown fond of each other. While they were out having a good time, Shakespeare stayed home alone writing sonnets and resolving never again to be so hasty about introducing friends. All we know about the dark lady is that she played the spinet, an obsolete kind of harpsichord which, in turn, was an obsolete kind of piano.* Otherwise she seems to have done nothing but keep the poet in a turmoil.†

In the end Shakespeare forgave the young man for having an affair with his mistress and vice versa. Upset as he may have been, he was able to conduct himself like a Renaissance gentleman and to express his feelings in the *abab cdcd efef gg* rhyme scheme as well as employ similes, metaphors, and alliteration.

Throughout the sonnets, Shakespeare lays bare his heart, and one gets an excellent view of the auricles and ventricles.

* *Cf. "They laughed when I sat down at the spinet. . . ."*
† *She was apparently married, though her husband doesn't come into the sonnets. But then neither does Shakespeare's wife.*

✎ Authorship of the Plays

Whoever wrote Shakespeare's plays, one thing is certain. It could not possibly have been Shakespeare. That would have been too obvious. Besides, the man had so little education that he could hardly read a play, much less write one. It is true that he might have attended school during the Lost Years, but if, as some believe, he was a schoolteacher at that time, he would have been far too busy teaching to learn anything. At any rate, it is a contemptible attack on higher education (an early instance of anti-intellectualism) to suggest that a person who never went to college could have written poetry that is too difficult for most college students.

Moreover, as anyone knows who has viewed the various Shakespeare signatures, if he had written the plays they would have been illegible.* Actors, given their parts in Shakespeare's

* *There seems to have been a flurry of progressive education at this time, and penmanship was on the decline. However quill pens, though not guaranteed to write under water, generally wrote very well on paper.*

handwriting, would have groped their way across the stage, overcome by emotion and eyestrain. Publication would have been impossible, unless the compositor was sufficiently creative to substitute poetry of his own for some undecipherable passage.

Obviously we must turn elsewhere for the authorship of Shakespeare's plays.

One person who may have written them is Francis Bacon, who had to be doing *something* when he wasn't serving as a Member of Parliament, acting as Solicitor-General, Attorney-General, and Lord Keeper,* and writing Bacon's *Complete Works.* If his own dull prose treatises and didactic essays are utterly unlike the imaginative poetry and inspired characterizations he wrote under the name of Shakespeare, it is indisputable proof that Bacon suffered not only from heartburn and Raleigh's Disease † but schizophrenia. Why Bacon chose the pen name ‡ of Shakespeare for his dramatic works is probably explained by his fear of what ham actors would do to plays under his own name. Also, he had said in one of his essays that "some books are to be chewed and digested." The librarians were after him, and he needed an alias.

Another person who may have written Shakespeare's plays is the Earl of Oxford. This gentleman had one advantage over Shakespeare when it came to writing plays: he had a title. Plots were everywhere,** but titles were hard to come by. Having lent his name to the University of Oxford, the Oxford Dictionary, the Oxford Movement, and a type of low brogan, the Earl thought it only fair to borrow someone else's name

* *Keeping lords was a full-time job itself.*
† *Brought on by antagonizing Queen Elizabeth.*
‡ *He was in the pen at the time, serving a term for bribery.*
** *See the Gunpowder Plot, etc.*

when he became a dramatist. Why he chose the name of Shakespeare is not known. Perhaps he closed his eyes and pointed at a name in the telephone book. Then again he may have liked the sound of the Oxford Edition of Shakespeare but felt that the Oxford Edition of Oxford would be overdoing it.

However the most likely author of Shakespeare's plays is Christopher Marlowe, who, having attended the University of Cambridge, had taken a course in Elizabethan Drama and knew all about tragic flaws, comic relief, etc. One thing that made it difficult for Marlowe to write Shakespeare's plays was the fact that he was killed in a tavern brawl before most of the plays were written.* Some maintain that Marlowe was not killed but only fatally wounded, lingering on for twenty years and writing as if each day were his last. Others believe that the later plays were written by Marlowe's descendants, often referred to as "Marlowe's mighty line." Still others contend that Marlowe wrote the plays in his tomb, where he could work uninterruptedly and be in close contact with the nether world. These researchers, who keep their ears to the ground and go into a frenzy whenever they think they hear the faint scratching of a quill, have been opening tombs and prying off coffin lids for years. The most recent tomb in which Marlowe was not discovered was that of his friend and protector, Sir Thomas Walsingham. But for the threatening inscription over the grave of William Shakespeare, Gent., of Stratford, they would long since have had the stones up, prepared to exclaim triumphantly to the figure rising from his writing desk, "Mr. Marlowe, I presume."

The time has not yet come to speak of the Age of Oxford or

* *And probably before paying his bill. See the Case of the Red Lion Inn vs. the Estate of Christopher Marlowe.*

the Baconian Theater, or to revise Shakespeare courses in college catalogues to read: "English 38a,b. Marlowe. Year course, 10 MWF . . . . English 142b. Advanced Marlowe. Second semester. 11 TThS." But one never knows.*

If, by chance, Shakespeare's works were not written by Bacon, the Earl of Oxford, or Marlowe, who could the author have been? Passing over the ingenious but inadequately documented cases recently made for the Piltdown Man, Whistler's Father, and Noel Coward, and brushing aside (with a large brush we keep for this purpose) the suggestion that it was Queen Elizabeth (who was really a man) or the Earl of Essex (who was really a woman), we come to a conclusion.

* *Does one?*